USA T*ODAY* BESTSELLING AUTHOR

Dale Mayer

TEEGAN 07

SHADOW RECON

TEEGAN: SHADOW RECON, BOOK 7
Beverly Dale Mayer
Valley Publishing Ltd.

ISBN-13: 978-1-778862-65-6
Print Edition

Books in This Series

Magnus, Book 1

Rogan, Book 2

Egan, Book 3

Barret, Book 4

Whalen, Book 5

Nikolai, Book 6

Teegan, Book 7

Mountain, Book 8

About This Book

Deep in the permafrost of the Arctic, a joint task force, comprised of over one dozen countries, comes together to level up their winter skills. A mix of personalities, nationalities, and egos bring out the best—and the worst—as these globally elite men and women work and play together. They rub elbows with hardy locals and a group of scientists gathered close by …

One fatality is almost expected with this training. A second is tough but not a surprise. However, when a third goes missing? It's hard to not be suspicious. When the missing man is connected to one of the elite Maverick team members and is a special friend of Lieutenant Commander Mason Callister? All hell breaks loose …

Battered and bruised, Teegan wakes up in the training camp struggling to remember the details of his last few weeks. But along with not knowing what happened to him, he also doesn't recognize the woman caring for him back in the camp. According to this Sandrine, he'd once asked her to marry him. Yet, he has no idea who she is…He didn't remember much about what happened, nor did he remember the woman looking after him. Sandrine that is. That information rolls through his confused brain along with the other disjointed bits of information he can't place, leaving him distrustful of everyone around him.

Sandrine can't believe the injured sick man in front of

her is Teegan. They had a history together but she'd not in any way thought she'd see him like this. He'd always been so fit and strong. All she wants is to get him back on his feet and be the man she used to know. But someone isn't done with him yet...

Teegan knows his brother is doing everything possible to solve these mysteries and to make sure no one gets a second chance to hurt him. But sometimes betrayal doesn't come from the outside... sometimes it comes from the inside... inside... and not outside...

PROLOGUE

TEEGAN OPENED HIS eyes, only to slam them shut against the bright light. He moaned ever-so-softly, as pain shivered through him. Gentle hands put a warm cloth against his forehead and gently wiped his face. "What happened?" he whispered.

"That'll be one of the questions I ask of you," a woman replied.

He opened his eyes to see a man standing there, looking ferocious, and a woman beside him, gently wiping his face. "Who are you?" he whispered.

"I'm Sydney. I'm the doctor here. I arrived not long after you disappeared."

He blinked at her several times and asked, "Where?"

At that, Mountain stepped forward. "Teegan, do you know who I am?"

He nodded. "Yeah, you're the guardian angel I've been praying for."

"Yeah, I'm here, brother. I'm just so damn sorry it took me so long to find you."

"I'm alive. That's what counts," he muttered, "but I sure as hell wish you could tell me what the hell happened."

"We'll get there. I'm not sure how much you remember or how much you'll ever remember," Mountain said, "but you're here now, and we'll protect you. You are the reason I came up here."

"Thank you for that," he added, as he opened his eyes. "Did you save the woman?"

"What woman?" Mountain asked, stepping forward.

"The one who was helping me."

"Was it Amelia?"

"Yes, Amelia."

"Why does she need saving?" Mountain asked, his voice choking up.

"She's the one who kept me alive. She's the one who kept moving me around to keep me alive," he shared, and then he winced. "Damn, it's really hard to keep a hold on the memories. Everything keeps shifting and mixing together."

At Teegan's side, Sydney turned to Mountain. "You'll need to give him a chance to rest and to get his thoughts together," she stated. "Everything'll be hazy, and, once again, we're dealing with the effects of that debilitating cold."

Mountain nodded. "I'll go get him a hot cup of tea."

At that, Teegan opened his eyes and stared at his brother. With a groan and a note of amusement in his voice, he said, "Tea? Really, bro? I would kill for a coffee just now."

Mountain looked over at Sydney, and she nodded. "Get him a coffee," she replied. "The stimulant won't hurt him at this point in time, and it might even help."

At that, Teegan whispered, "Christ, if only I could get warm."

"We'll get you warm," the doc declared, "I see a touch of frostbite on your toes. But that should heal in time."

He nodded. "Yeah, I don't remember how or where."

Mountain glanced to the other bed. "And, Jesus Christ, somebody needs to fill me in on what the hell happened to

Carl."

Teegan looked over at Mountain. "You need to find Amelia."

"I'll find her," Mountain promised, "but we need to sort you out first."

Then a knock came on the clinic door, and another woman stepped in. She looked over at Sydney. "Doctor? I'm Sandrine," she stated. "I'm a nurse and came in on the supply plane. I understand you've been a little over-whelmed."

"Yeah, you could say that," Sydney admitted. "I had somebody helping, but she's been quite sick."

"I'm not, and I'm here and ready to help wherever I can." She walked over to Teegan, then looked at him and winced. "Teegan?"

He raised heavy eyelids and stared at her in confusion. "Sorry, do I know you?"

Disappointment crossed her face, and then she shrugged. She looked over at Sydney and masked her features in an instant. "What can I do to help?"

Noticing the unmistakable hurt in her voice, Sydney smiled at her. "Teegan's come back from an extremely rough ordeal, and we don't know the details yet," she explained. "Unfortunately neither does he. His memories aren't there, and he doesn't have any recollection of what's happened to him. Please don't take offense to anything he says right now."

Sandrine looked at her in shock.

Teegan opened his eyes. "I still don't remember you, but the doc's right. Everything is hazy, and I'm far from 100 percent. Sorry, I'm not trying to insult you."

"That's fine," she replied gently, as she looked at him. "I

won't take it personally then."

"I gather I know you?"

"You could say so," she stated. "At one point in time, you asked me to marry you."

DAY 1

TEEGAN RODE WOKE with a start, his gaze blurry and the room around him in shadows. His heart slammed against his chest, and his breath caught in the back of his throat. It was all he could do to manage to get a breath out, only to panic that somebody had heard him. He lay quietly, desperate to calm down his breathing, when he realized he was lying on something soft, and he was warm. For the first time in a very long time he was toasty warm. Something covered him, and that was an otherworldly sensation. It was the best news he'd had for … He couldn't remember how long, and, on that matter, his mind went completely blank.

He shifted uneasily, hating the fear of not knowing what had happened, where he was, or placing anything in his memory banks where they belonged. He had recognized his brother, but he hadn't recognized the doctor, and he certainly hadn't recognized the one called Sandrine. Fear ate away at the back of his brain. Hating the thought, but it was there. *That he might have imagined Mountain.* Even then, he stared down at his fingers, realizing he was on a real bed, gripping real sheets. He clinched his fingers as hard as he could, trying to burn up some of his nervous energy, as he tried to reassess where and who he was.

A woman, her voice gentle in the darkness, whispered, "You're fine, Teegan. This is Sandrine, and I'm sitting here beside you. You are not alone." Then a hand gently covered his tight fists. "It's okay to relax."

He opened his eyes again, staring up at the woman. He whispered, "Where am I?" She didn't say anything for a moment, and he looked at her, curious. Then he started to shiver, his actions belying what he previously thought was warmth. With a startled exclamation, she quickly switched out his blanket for something much warmer. He shuddered underneath it and groaned.

"It's okay. This will pass too," she replied in a soothing voice.

He kept his eyelids closed, as he shifted to his side, wincing at more pain.

"In case you don't know," she began, her voice calm in his ear, "you have sores on your side, as if you'd been lying on that side for too long. So any kind of movement will hurt them. You're on painkillers, but we're trying to limit that because you're so cold, and we can't have your vitals dropping any further."

He shifted and asked in a whisper, "Does anybody know what happened?"

"Nope, but everybody's hoping you'll tell us." Leaning closer, she added, "That's not a worry right now. You just focus on getting better. Close your eyes, and go back to sleep, if you can."

That happened several times, despite how hard he tried, desperate to stay awake. He drifted off again, woke up, shifted, groaned in pain, but found her always there, comforting in a way. Then he rolled over and went to sleep again. When he woke up for the umpteenth time, Sandrine wasn't there. He shifted anxiously, feeling something missing in his world.

Another woman arrived, the doctor, the one who called herself Sydney. She smiled at him. "Hey."

"Sandrine?" he whispered.

"She's gone to lie down." The doc nodded in understanding. "She's been here, looking after you all night. I told her to go get some rest."

He gave a half nod, then closed his eyes, grateful that Sandrine was okay and still around, which was completely different from what his mind had jumped to, which had her in trouble. He didn't know how long it would take for all these disjointed thoughts and nightmares to calm down, but, if this night was anything to go by, it would still be quite a while.

When he woke the next time, he shifted in bed and looked over at the doctor, who sat at a desk far off to the side.

As soon as she noticed his movements, she got up and stepped over to take a look at him. "Hey." She automatically checked his vitals. "Glad to see you're awake."

"I think I'm awake this time," he muttered, yawning.

"How are you feeling temperature-wise?" She checked his body temperature and frowned.

"Still chilled," he replied, "but doing better."

She nodded. "You are doing better, though you're still colder than I would like, but, hey, that's almost par for the course up here." She smiled as she peered down at him. "A lot of people are waiting to talk to you."

He nodded. "Any chance of food first?"

Her face lit up. "Wanting food is good. I'll get someone to …"

Then the door opened, and Mountain walked in, and whatever the doc was getting at was left unsaid. Mountain had a big smile on his face, when Teegan turned to look at him.

"Hey, Mountain." Teegan flashed him a smile. "I thought I might have imagined you at one point. Not sure what I ever did to deserve a brother like you, but trust me. … You'll be on my Christmas list forever."

Mountain burst out laughing. "That'll be a change," he teased affectionately.

He looked relieved, but Teegan recognized that look in his brother's eyes—one of fear, pain, and, at the same time, joy. "It's not your fault, bro."

"You sure about that?" Mountain asked, as he reached for Teegan's hand and picked it up gently. "Doc's still not very happy with your condition."

"Yeah, I got that." Teegan shifted and then groaned in pain again.

Mountain glanced over at Sydney in concern. She walked over to face him. "He needs food, but I also need to change his dressings. We'll do the food afterward because changing the dressings will hurt like shit," she shared. "You'll have to wait because he'll need to sleep off the pain, and then you'll have a chance to talk to him afterward."

Mountain frowned at her, and she shook her head. "Dressings first, then he gets coffee and food, and we'll see if he can hold it down and stay awake. I'll give him something for pain after that," she added. "It is what it is, so deal with it."

"Or you can give him painkillers first, so the pain of the dressing change isn't quite so bad."

She gave him a quick glance and then snapped, "Listen. My job is in here. Your job is out there. So, you better leave, go do you, and leave me here to do my thing."

When Mountain fisted his hands on his hips, she took one step forward and did the same, then cranked her head back so she could glare up at him. "Go. And don't you dare try pulling any of those strong-arm tactics on me," she snapped.

Teegan watched both of them in fascination because Mountain being schooled like that was quite a rare occurrence.

Looking as if he was teetering on the brink of explosion, Mountain finally groaned. "Jeez, you're always so feisty."

"Yeah? You haven't seen half of it yet," Sydney declared, as she held the door open for him. "Go get him a coffee, and knock before you come back in, so we can be sure I've got the dressings changed."

Teegan wasn't sure what the undercurrents were on that one, but he was getting the impression that changing the dressings wouldn't be something he liked. Still, he lay here, as she checked him over from head to toe once again. "How bad is it?"

"You've got some bedsores. They cause you pain when you try to move. You've also got frostbite on a couple of toes, though your fingers are doing better than I expected. Overall, considering what you've been through, and the fact that you could be far worse, as in dead," she stated bluntly, "you're doing pretty well. Now the skin isn't healing as it should because it hasn't had any chance to," she added. "As much as I've tried to keep you off those bedsores, you keep shifting in your sleep, so you end up lying on them."

He looked at her in confusion. "How come I can't feel them?"

She nodded. "I've been using a numbing cream to get you through the night, but, according to Sandrine, you woke up multiple times."

And, for the last however many days, he had woken up multiple times in the night. "Yeah, I get it, but where are these sores?"

"Your feet, your butt, your back, and your belly. If I can get you to roll over, I'll start changing dressings."

"I did wake up often, but I don't know if it was pain that kept waking me up or not."

"It probably was, even if you didn't recognize it as such," she agreed.

Feeling his body burning from top to bottom, he was thankful when the doc used the cream again, and it started to help pretty quickly.

With a lot of effort and her assistance, he soon found himself lying on his belly, with his back exposed, and he felt the chill creeping up on him.

She gave him two hand warmers. "Hold on to these, but I've got to get these dressings changed. Hold on, and I'll get it sorted as quickly as I can."

And that started a marathon of pain, cleaning, and new bandages, and in between that was cold, shivers, and blankets covering him from time to time, so as not to exhaust him with all the shaking going on.

When she finally had him all cleaned up, she rolled him over once again and took care of the scrapes on his belly. "I'll leave you on your back for a few minutes, while I check the front."

He stared at her in horror. "You mean, there's more?" He hated to think that this could be worse, but, dammit, it was way worse. She gave him something to bite down on for the next round, as she went to his hips, plus one knee was in rough shape. He could see enough of the red marks all over him, but she checked every inch of him thoroughly.

When she was finally satisfied, she noted, "Okay, let's get you covered up and on the road to warm again. Then you can have coffee, and, if that goes well, we can get some food for you …"

By the time he was tucked in and seated more upright on the hospital bed, at least enough that he was reasonably comfortable and taking the pressure off the bedsores, he groaned. "I guess that's why I kept flipping around overnight."

"I've been trying to get you to stay face down. I don't have any straps here. However, not knowing what you've been through, I didn't want to strap you down in case you woke up with horrific nightmares or something and started to freak out," she explained. "I'm hoping now that you're more alert and aware of where all the pain is coming from and why, we can start shifting you constantly to let some of this heal up." Motioning to her own back to point out where most of the sores were, she went on. "Honestly, I would love to have some of these wounds open to the air, so they could get a chance to dry out."

When he looked at her in horror, she nodded. "Sorry, but it is a necessary evil, and I really do think it will help. However, I need to consider the process for that. In the meantime, we have to deal with the fact that your body temperature can't stay regulated, and you'll need a bit more time to warm up." She frowned, deeply focused on some internal thoughts. "Food is important. Your brother is here with coffee, so I'll let him in, if you're okay to see him."

Teegan stared at her with glazed eyes. "Coffee would be nice, but damn."

"I know," she muttered. She patted him on the shoulder,

then walked over and pulled open the door.

From his vantage point, Teegan could see Sandrine walking down the hallway with Mountain standing there, talking on his phone.

Sydney let them both in, reminding them both with the warning, "He's not in great shape at the moment," she shared in a low tone. "No questions." Mountain glared at her, and she gave him a flat stare back.

"We'll see," Mountain grumbled.

As soon as he stepped in, Teegan watched his brother's expression change to one of concern. "I'm fine," Teegan muttered. "I didn't realize there were so many wounds."

"What kind of wounds?" Mountain asked, turning to face Sydney.

She shrugged. "Aside from the frostbite, some are scrapes that have gotten infected. Some look as if they could be the result of attempts at escape, though I don't know. Some of the worse are bedsores from staying in the same position for too long."

As Mountain stared at her in shock, she nodded. "We can have a talk about this afterward, but he's had his dressings changed and his wounds cleaned up, so I don't want to keep Teegan up. ... He might need to sleep for a bit. I gave him painkillers, but I know that he's probably burning from head to toe right now."

Teegan shifted uneasily in the bed, only to feel ripples of anguish once again run up and down his body. He whispered, "Didn't somebody say there was coffee?"

Mountain snapped out of his shock and stepped forward, placing the cup beside Teegan, then moved the little table close enough so his brother could reach it. "Dammit, Teegan."

Teegan gave him a half smile. "You found me. That's a win."

"Yeah, I'm not so sure you were found as much as maybe you were given back to us as a gift," he muttered. Teegan stared at him, but Mountain shook his head. "We'll talk about it later." Mountain's anguish and frustration were evident in his tone. "I do need you to think hard about anything at all you can remember, anything you can tell me, so we can find out who did this to you."

"Did you find Amelia?"

"No, I have not found Amelia." Then he hesitated and admitted, "Honestly, I haven't gone looking. I've been here with you."

Teegan glared at him. "You have to help her."

"I said I would, but she's obviously very capable of dealing with this type of situation."

"She's doing her best, but she's hurt," Teegan shared.

At that, Mountain looked up, startled. "You didn't say she was hurt."

"I didn't? I suppose I haven't had much chance," he muttered. "Am I even all here?" he asked, as he shivered some more. "I can't keep a single thread of thought straight."

Mountain picked up the slightly cooled coffee and held it to Teegan's lips. He took several sips, before settling back and sighing with pleasure. "Nothing quite like a cup of coffee after doing without."

"Yeah, but the question is, why you had to do without." Mountain noted, staring at his brother. "None of this makes any sense."

"Oh, I'm sure it does. We don't have the pieces to the puzzle yet," Sydney stated at his side.

Mountain nodded. "And I need answers, and he's the

one who can give them to me."

"I understand that, but you will not hound him," Sydney stated, her tone completely inflexible. "You can talk to him as long as he's capable, but I don't want to see you exhausting him. His body is way too weak for us to work to get him to this point, only to have to start over and to fight for his body to get stronger again. So, here's the deal. … You can talk but not to the point of his being overwhelmed. I will kick you out of here if it comes to that."

At that, Teegan nodded toward the cup, and Mountain picked it up and held it for him. This time, Teegan managed to grasp it with both hands, almost moaning in delight at the warmth of the cup itself. He huddled with the cup close to his mouth and sipped it constantly.

When he'd had enough, he handed it back to his brother and whispered, "Thanks." Catching sight of Mountain's frown, Teegan attempted to give him a reassuring smile, though it must have come across as more of a twisted caricature, if his brother's expression was anything to go by. "Honestly, I'm doing okay," he murmured.

"Yeah, you're doing okay, meaning you're alive," Mountain said, "but you're in rough shape, with some brain fog. Plus you're frozen, and you're pretty well beat-up."

"I don't have X-ray capabilities here," Sydney explained to Teegan, "but I'll guess that you have a couple cracked ribs, potentially a cracked fibula, some muscle damage, a burn from a bullet along your ribs, and several soft-tissue injuries. Most are healing. Some swelling appears still in various places. Oh, and I can see an attempt at stitches on your head that have since healed, and the stitches removed. It was damn hard to find, so whoever did it did a good job. That also explains the memory loss. As would drugs, trauma, and many other considerations."

Sydney continued, now addressing Mountain. "No obvious internal injuries that I can find so far, and Teegan is eating, which is a good sign, although I'll definitely restrict what he eats."

At that, Teegan looked at her in horror, as she nodded. "I need to confirm you can keep it down."

"So, what will you give me then? Because, right about now, I could really go for a steak."

Her lips twitched. "Nope, no steak, but maybe we can start with some scrambled eggs, unless you would rather have oatmeal."

He frowned at her. "Oatmeal is fine, as long as it comes with lots of nuts and fresh cream," he murmured. "I don't know what I have as an option."

"I'll get you something," Sydney offered. "Remember. It'll be a little something to start with." He glared at her, and she nodded. "I know, and you can get as pissed off as you want. Once I see this stay down, you can have more." With that, she looked at Mountain. "Can you stay here for a few minutes, while I get him food?"

He nodded. "Go. I'll watch over him."

As soon as she was gone, Mountain looked down at Teegan. "She won't let me ask you any questions," he said, nearly growling.

"Since when does that make a difference to you?" Teegan would have laughed if he'd had the energy but gave Mountain a half smile instead, and that was as good as it got. Damn, he had the best brother. "What happened here while I was gone?"

"Well, … that would be a lot. Amelia went missing. We didn't know what happened to you, and we're missing a lot of information."

"So nobody knows what the hell's going on in this place, correct?"

"Yeah, you got it." Mountain shook his head. "I've never seen anything like it."

"I think that you don't understand who's involved."

"That is true. I don't. Are you saying that you do?"

"No. When I was held captive, I didn't know who or what was going on. I wasn't conscious most of the time, and I was given drugs of some kind," he added, pointing to his arm.

At that, Mountain stepped closer and gently took one of Teegan's arms clutched up against his chest, and slowly straightened it out, until he could see the tracks of needle marks. A lot of needle marks. He swore at that. A couple were infected.

"Yeah, how do you think I feel? I also don't know how much this has to do with my memory issues now too."

Trying to keep his cool, Mountain took a deep breath. "Do you remember what you were doing before you disappeared?"

"No." Teegan frowned. "Why did they contact you anyway?"

"In a way, you contacted me. You knew you were in danger."

Teegan stared up at him in shock. "I did?"

"You did," Mountain confirmed. "The trouble is, you didn't seem to have any idea of how or what you could do to help yourself, and you were reaching out."

"What was I doing?"

"You were investigating the questionable accidents going on here. And you had some proof of how all of them could have been intentionally arranged, not accidents at all. But you didn't provide any of that proof for us to go on."

Teegan stared up at him, blinking several times, as he tried to process the information. He sagged back against the bed and shook his head. "It doesn't make any sense."

"Yeah, that would be our take on it too," Mountain agreed, with a humorous note. "You can expect to see the colonel here pretty soon as well."

"I hope it's not too soon because I don't have any answers, and I really don't want to get barked at."

"You might not get barked at," Mountain shared, "but don't forget that you are still military and assigned to this training base, so you will answer to him."

"Of course," Teegan muttered. "Yet, at the moment, I just, … honest to God, bro, I don't have a clue."

"That's also concerning," Mountain noted, as he stared around the room. "Did you have anybody you were afraid of? Anything triggering that right now?"

Teegan snorted.

Mountain looked down at him, his lips twitching. "Okay, so *afraid* may not be the right word," he clarified, with a grin. "Was there anybody you would be concerned about, say, catching you in the dark or attacking you from the back? Anyone hunting you, stalking you, watching you too closely, saying something sideways, commenting to somebody else about you? Anything or anybody at all who would give me something to go on?"

Teegan shook his head. "Not right now, not that I can think of." Teegan sighed. "Maybe if I get a chance to relax enough and to heal enough, some of it will pop back up again."

Silence came for a long moment, and then Mountain

asked him, "What about this Sandrine? Did you get to the point to remember her?"

"I don't remember her," Teegan said. "I wanted to ask you if I really did know her." He hesitated then added, "But there's a feeling of … I don't know… maybe familiarity. A warmth that's hard to explain."

"Interesting. Yet you don't remember her specifically."

At that, the door opened, and Sydney walked in. She looked at the two of them inquiringly, as she carried the tray of food inside. "Problems?"

"I was asking about Sandrine," Teegan replied.

Sydney nodded. "Yeah, I want to know where you knew her from as well."

Mountain added, "That's the thing. He doesn't remember."

"Maybe we should be asking Sandrine then," Sydney suggested, and Mountain nodded.

"Agreed," Mountain replied, with an odd suspicion weaving through his voice.

In perfect timing, Sandrine walked in then, glaring at him. "You're welcome to ask me anything you want," she stated, looking at both Sydney and Mountain. She walked over to Teegan. She reached out a hand, placing it gently on his shoulder, saying, "Hey. How're you doing?"

Teegan looked up, feeling something settle inside him, now that she was here again. "I'm fine," he replied, with a sigh. "I'm awake, and I made it through the night, though I'm pretty sure I owe a lot of that to you."

"No, not to me at all," she disagreed. "That was you fighting the battles out there."

"What do you mean?" Mountain asked, stepping forward and glaring at them.

"Nightmares," she noted, turning to look at him. "Lots of them. He was calling out and fighting off demons of some kind in whatever nightmare scenario he was caught up in."

"Did he say anything?" Mountain asked sharply.

She blinked at him and then slowly shook her head. "Nothing that I would have considered important."

"It's all important," he bit off. "I need to know absolutely everything he said."

She turned to look at Sydney, and the doc nodded. "He needs to know. You didn't mention that when I came in this morning."

"I didn't think it was important. He called out a couple times in the night." She turned to look at Teegan. "It wasn't specific names or dates, or 'Hey, stop kidnapping me,' or anything such as that. There was a lot of *No*, and *Leave me alone*, and lots of crying out for Mountain, which I didn't even realize was your name, until Sydney told me," Sandrine explained.

Mountain nodded. "I'm glad he was calling out for me."

"Why is that?" she asked, looking over at him. "Wouldn't it be better if he was calling out for help or something?"

"That's what he was doing when he was calling for me. Our family is tightly knit. As soon as I realized he'd gone missing, I came." Mountain looked over at Sandrine. "When did you arrive here?"

"I came in with the latest supplies—yesterday. The investigator Samson, he already questioned me, and I've been cleared."

"I'll have to talk to him," Mountain added, with a thoughtful look.

"Oh, I'm pretty sure he's looking to talk to you, and

definitely Teegan too."

Mountain nodded. "After I leave here, I'll go track him down."

"You can, but I got the impression he might be heading out to do some reconnaissance on his own." At that, Mountain turned and stared. She shrugged. "Look. I don't know anything. I spent all night here with Teegan, trying to get him through the night. I'm glad that he's doing much better now. I came to relieve Sydney, if she needed to go get some breakfast." She looked down at the tray that Sydney had placed on the table. "Oh, did you pick up breakfast?"

"No, I brought some for Teegan."

"Oh good. Let's hope he can keep it down."

"Did he upchuck in the night?" the doc asked.

"No, but it wasn't a sound sleep."

"In that case, we'll definitely feed him bland foods to start," Sydney noted.

"I can feed myself," Teegan replied, trying to listen to the conversation, but it was moving quickly, and his head was already starting to hurt. "However, if I don't eat soon, I'll be asleep." With that, he shifted in the bed and barely held back a cry of pain.

Sydney walked over and suggested, "Let's get some food into you." She turned to Mountain. "Go ahead and take off, if you need to track down the investigator. I'll talk to you in a bit, and, if anything changes, I'll contact you."

He hesitated, as if not really wanting to leave Teegan's side.

When she raised one eyebrow, he gave a clipped nod and walked out.

SANDRINE LOOKED OVER at Sydney. "You don't seem to be intimidated by him."

"Nope, he's worried about his brother. Mountain would never cross a line, unless it was to save somebody who was important to him," she shared, with a knowing smile. "In this case, I know perfectly well that Teegan's important, and luckily Teegan knows that all too well."

As she walked over with the food tray, she placed it beside Teegan. "Now let's see if we can get some food down you." He lifted up a hand, and she shook her head. "Nope, way too much effort. I'll help you."

"May I?" Sandrine asked, stepping up to the side.

Sydney hesitated, then nodded and looked at Teegan. "Sure, unless you have a problem with it?"

He shook his head. "Nobody should feed me," he stated, with a hopeful glance. "I'm sure I can do it myself."

"But it will take effort and energy, which you don't have to spare right now," the doc replied. "So, the answer is no."

He groaned. "Fine. Fine, okay. I got the message." And, with that, he looked over at Sandrine. "I guess you're on baby-feeding duty."

She laughed, pulled up a chair, picked up a spoonful of oatmeal, and teased, "Open up then. Here comes the choo-choo."

With a strangled laugh, Teegan obediently opened his mouth. She smiled, as she continued to feed him, until half the bowl was gone. But almost from one moment to the next, he shook his head. "I'm done. That's plenty."

She looked down at the amount, and Sydney walked over, took a look, and nodded. "That's probably a safe amount anyway. Now, why don't you try to get some sleep."

He shifted in the bed and whispered, "I need to roll

over."

"We can help you do that."

And, with Sandrine and Sydney on either side, they got Teegan rolled over, until he was flat, his head turned to the side, lying on his belly.

Sandrine covered him up again, then leaned over and whispered, "Do you need anything else?"

"Sleep," he mumbled. Then he drifted off.

Sandrine picked up the tray with the food bowl and the coffee cup and asked, "Are you okay if I return this to the kitchen?"

Sydney nodded. "Go get yourself something too."

"How did you know I didn't eat already?"

"I feel as if I already got the message here on you and Teegan," Sydney shared. "I don't know where your relationship is at or what happened," she noted, "but clearly you still care for him."

She looked back at the man in the bed. "Caring was never the issue," she muttered, with a wistful smile.

Walking to the dining room and then into the kitchen, Sandrine took care of the dishes, quickly scraping away the remainder of the food.

Elijah, the chef, walked over and asked, "How's he doing?"

"He ate half the oatmeal and drank the coffee, but now he's out cold again."

Elijah nodded. "Hey, at least he's alive."

"You're not kidding," she murmured, looking over at him. "I don't suppose any breakfast is left? I don't think Sydney's eaten either."

Chef frowned at that. "The kitchen is pretty-well done with breakfast. Both of you were late."

"I know. We were looking after Teegan."

He nodded. "I've got an omelet ready for you," he replied. "It's big, so I cut it in half, and I've got some other leftovers from breakfast for you."

Surprised to see a tray already set aside for them, she asked him, "How did you know I would be by to get it?"

He laughed. "If you didn't come by, I planned to take it down," he shared. "No point in saving this and letting it go to waste." He gave her a headshake.

She grinned. "You're a good guy."

"Sometimes." He nodded. "Sometimes."

Sandrine picked up the tray, thinking about his comment, how so many of the men here were all about helping others and being the ones here to solve problems, but sometimes that worked, and sometimes it didn't. She had had some uncomfortable conversations herself, after arriving here, not even knowing that Teegan was here. Yet now that she did know, it was hard for her to do anything but stay by his side.

Of course she came to help, but that didn't mean she would get the opportunity to stick close. As she walked into the medical clinic, Sydney was getting off the phone. "Chef sent down breakfast for both of us. Apparently he didn't like the fact that you didn't show up for breakfast either."

Sydney laughed. "Yeah, he's got this thing about making sure none of us starve."

"It's a good thing though," Sandrine noted. "Apparently he had already done a head count or taken attendance somehow and realized that we hadn't eaten. I did ask him what he would do if we hadn't shown up at all."

Sydney interjected, "Oh, he would have delivered the food himself. He's very good at that and always shows up wherever he is needed, ... kind of like a mother hen," she stated, with a half smile.

Sandrine set down the tray and handed off one plate to the doc.

"Thanks, I'll eat a bite while I can." Sydney was already digging into her omelet.

Sandrine nodded, looking over at Teegan. "Is he still asleep?"

"He is," the doc confirmed, "and, when he was awake, he seemed to be fine with you. I need to know that whatever history is between you two won't set back his progress, when he does remember who you are." She had another bite of her eggs.

"I don't know," Sandrine admitted. "I can't imagine that there would be anything so drastic. We haven't seen each other in a few years."

Syndey finished off half of her omelet, then set down her fork. "And yet you mentioned how he asked you to marry him. That's hardly setting me on a course to speculate about anything good."

"He did ask me to marry him, and we had been going out for a while, but I don't think his question was serious by any means—or I guess I should say I don't really know how serious he was. He did ask me though," she stated, with a half smile. "At the time, I put it down more to the alcohol than to his caring that much. I knew he cared. I just didn't think he cared that much, so I took it as a joke."

"So now, do you still feel the same? After all this time, in hindsight, ... do you think it was a joke?"

"Yes, absolutely," she declared, facing the doc. "Would I have turned him down if it wasn't a joke? I don't have an answer for that question." Then she laughed. "Everybody always wants to know how things such as that happen, and sometimes it just … does. You don't even know what you're doing, but, the next thing you know, somebody's mouthing off and making a comment."

"Maybe that's his personality," Sydney suggested.

"Maybe. But whatever it was, it was left at that, and he headed off on a mission. After that, he was posted to Germany for a while, and we lost track of each other. In the meantime, everything kind of dissipated."

"Are you sad about that?"

"Meaning, am I still holding a torch for him or whatever?" she asked, with amusement. "No, I'm not. He's a nice guy, and I really cared about him and for him. He was quite a sweetheart," she shared, with a chuckle. "But that doesn't mean I've been sitting around, waiting for him to come back. I'm not that kind of a fool."

"I'm not sure it's even being foolish," Sydney replied, studying Sandrine.

"It sure didn't do me any good to wait around," Sandrine explained, "because, after Germany, I don't know where he went, but he didn't contact me."

Sydney's gaze was intense, and then she relaxed. "Military life is rough on everybody."

"It's definitely rough on relationships," Sandrine agreed, with a small smile. "I've seen more divorces and more hookups and breakups than I care to remember."

"How is it you ended up coming here?" Sydney asked.

Sandrine shrugged. "I'm not even sure. They were looking for somebody to do nursing support on short notice. I've never been one to shy away from a challenge. I was part of the conversation, or nearby more precisely, when I heard about the opportunity, and I said I would be interested in going." As she spoke, she walked over and adjusted Teegan's blanket.

"To me, it is quite obvious that you still care," Sydney shared.

Sandrine shrugged. "We had fun together." She gave a gentle smile to the man who had stolen her heart. "I knew that it wouldn't be for a long time. You know that old song? *We're here for a good time, not a long time?*" she asked, with a sad smile.

With a commiserating smile, Sydney asked, "Are you okay to stay here for a while? I've got a meeting this morning."

"Sure." Sandrine gave a slight nod. "Do you want me to contact you if he wakes up?"

"No, just keep him quiet, but, if he's in a lot of pain, … then you can contact me," Sydney added. "I need to supervise his medication."

"Sure, that makes sense." Sandrine nodded, understanding the need here, what with Teegan already pumped full of drugs by his kidnapper.

She sat down to wait beside Teegan's bed, while Sydney packed up a few things and then quickly walked out. The clinic felt strange without her. It was very much Sydney's space, her dominion, and, based on everything Sandrine had heard, Sydney was a hell of a doctor and had worked hard to keep everybody here doing well. Sandrine hoped that Teegan would be fine, and certainly it appeared that way, but she also knew that some of these cases could turn around on a dime when complications arose.

She didn't necessarily know what Teegan's problem was, but he was certainly in significant pain, and she could imagine that getting him out of here would be a primary discussion at that meeting. She didn't know if anybody could make it happen, but Mountain would certainly be working at it, if he could.

Teegan woke up once and stared at her.

She patted his hand and whispered, "I'm here. Go back to sleep."

Without any complaint, he'd rolled over and closed his eyes.

He seemed to have an easier time rolling to the left than he did on the right, but, as she mentally reviewed the wounds on his body, it made sense.

Sandrine had been horrified when she'd seen the initial set of wounds she had helped dress, and even Sydney had gone very silent and hadn't said much, focusing on the job at hand.

When they were finally done, the doc had turned to Sandrine and whispered, "Don't speak to anyone about any of this."

Sandrine nodded. "I wasn't planning on it."

"Everything you see in here is to be considered top secret," Sydney declared. "I am not sure what the hell's going on, but he has suffered way more than anybody should ever have to."

Teegan looked so much older to Sandrine, due to his kidnapping and his injuries, plus he had lost a lot of weight. And, even now, he looked almost haggard, as his world had been a harsh and unwelcoming place for the last many weeks. And, from what Sandrine had gathered from conversations that nobody was prepared to fill her in on, Teegan had been missing for quite a while. Even now, nobody knew quite where he'd been or what had happened to him out there in the Arctic tundra.

She couldn't imagine it, since Teegan was one of those capable, well-thought-of, popular young men who, she knew, would always be *that guy*. That guy who was invited to the parties. That guy who would always be a best man for his buddies, would always be there when somebody needed them, whether helping to build a deck or babysitting in a pinch. He was definitely *that guy*. He was the one you could count on and always had a smile on his face.

She stared down at him and whispered, "Teegan, whatever happened to us?"

He didn't answer, and she wouldn't have asked if she'd thought that he could hear her, but she'd often wondered where he'd gone and what his life had ended up being. To find that the two of them were both in this place now? Well, she was a nurse and had done a lot of traveling around the world herself, and it had been a lot of fun.

She hadn't been ready to settle down back then, but now? She was getting to the point where she was wondering what she wanted to do next and wondering whether she wanted to keep doing this or potentially head into a different kind of practice. Her mother was a pediatrician, and her father worked in the same private clinic where her mother worked, and they were both pushing to bring Sandrine into the same company.

She'd often thought of it, wondering if she was ready for that change, but she didn't know. It had been an interesting few years, hopping around the world, and change was a good thing, but her future wasn't something she would think about right now. It was a decision for down the road. Although, as she looked at Teegan, she wondered if maybe the change she needed was to find a partner, to start a family, to settle down and relax. She wanted to have those kids that she'd always expected to already have at this stage of life.

She was a little bit behind schedule, if there was a sched-ule for something such as this, but she always thought that, by the time she was thirty, she would have settled down and been pregnant, if not already having one child. They say that, for women, the prime age range would be twenty-five to thirty-five for having kids, although a lot of older women were having babies now.

Lost in her thoughts, she didn't see that Teegan had opened his eyes. He reached out and brushed her hand, and she blinked several times as she registered him staring up at her. She smiled. "Hey." Sandrine automatically reached for the water beside her and offered him a drink with the straw.

He sipped the water and relaxed back. "Is it just us here?" he asked.

"It is for the moment," she said, with a nod. "Sydney's gone to a meeting. I'm not sure where your brother is, but he's probably out … terrorizing the world or something."

His lips twitched, and he nodded. "That's Mountain. He's the guy to have at your side, if and when something ever blows up."

"Did you really leave a message for him or something?"

"I don't remember," Teegan admitted, "but, if I thought I was in danger, which apparently I was, … I would have done everything I could to have brought him on board. Nothing like having Mountain's help."

"Except you," she pointed out. "Apparently you're a chip off the old block."

"A smaller chip off that same block maybe," he replied, laughing softly. "Mountain and I have always been close. He's a good guy, the best, and one of the most capable men I've ever known." Teegan sighed, then closed his eyes. "So, who knows? The fact that he found me is amazing, though I don't even know what the circumstances were." He shook his head. "I know from the pain, ... whatever I've been through," he muttered, "it wasn't pretty."

"Do you remember being injected with needles?"

He nodded. "That I can remember. ... I'm not sure who did it. Or why."

"So, they never told you, *huh?*"

"No, not that I ever heard anything. I remember asking him why he was doing it and what he wanted out of it, and, at one point in time, I thought there was an apology, ... but I could be wrong."

"An apology?" she asked, settling back and staring at him. "That's an odd thing."

"I know. That's why I'm not sure I even heard it," he shared, opening his eyes to stare up at her. "That's the problem right now. Everything is weaving in and out, and it doesn't seem to be anything I can count on. I know I need to talk to the investigators and to give them every bit of information I possibly can. I don't really know what that is."

"Give them the truth. And definitely tell them that you're not sure how much of it is even something they can depend on. But they must have something to go on, and you're the only one who appears to have something to give them, anything at all to give them."

"I wish they'd found Amelia."

Her heart did a slow burn at the mention of this woman whom Teegan sounded so smitten with. "I'm sorry, particularly when she seems to have done so much for you."

"Exactly." Teegan shifted again. "She's a special woman."

Sandrine nodded, a little bit numbly. "Of course she is,"

she replied, faking a warm response. "I'm glad you found someone so special."

He blinked at her and asked, "What are you talking about?"

Sandrine frowned. "Didn't you know her before?"

"No, not at all," he stated, staring at her. "She … she was the one who rescued me. But I don't know where she rescued me from and even if it actually was a rescue." He groaned, as he sank back. "God, what a mess."

"But we have you, and you're safe. So whatever the mess is, now it can be sorted out."

His lips twitched, as he rolled his head to the side and focused on her. "I have to admit it is lovely to wake up and to see your smiling face," he whispered, with half a smile, yet still sad. "Honestly, it was like a homing beacon in the night, and, when you weren't there when I woke up this morning, I was almost frantic, trying to figure out where I was." As she stared at him, trying to sort out what he meant, he explained. "The doc was here, but you weren't."

"Ah, yes. I was sent to rest up for a bit, since I'd been up all night," she admitted.

"Sorry about that," he said.

"Don't be," she murmured. "I wanted to stay and to ensure you were okay. That was paramount."

"It's appreciated. I hadn't realized how torn up and destroyed my dreams were, but apparently all I could see during the night were horrible scenarios."

"Which is to be expected, but it's fine," she said. "I was happy to stay and to look after you."

"I presume you're a nurse, or are you a doctor or—"

"A nurse," she replied, with a nod. "And, in case you don't remember, which I gather you don't, we knew each other a few years back."

"Did I really ask you to marry me?"

She laughed and stated, "Yes, you did."

"Wow. I must have been a real jerk for you to turn me down."

She couldn't stop laughing at that. "Honestly, I didn't think the proposal was even serious at the time. I think you were more drunk than anything."

"Ooh, ouch," he muttered. "You should never propose to a woman when you're drunk," he noted, with a grimace. "It's definitely not in the guidebook about how to get yourself hitched."

She started to laugh. "My God," she said, all grins and smiles. "I'm not doubting that such a book could exist, not in the world we live in," she added, "but you're right. I don't think that would be considered a good move."

"Well, yeah, how would anybody ever know if you were sincere if you were drunk?"

"Hence my problem," she replied, chuckling.

It was so good to see him laughing and joking, talking normally, and even looking at the world as if he were on the mend, that she allowed herself to relax and to remember the guy he used to be. And while he clearly wasn't the same, yet, in a way, he almost was. She kept catching insights into the guy he used to be, little ways that he moved his head, things that he mentioned, the way he said it. The old Teegan Rode was in there somewhere.

When the door opened a little bit later, and both Mountain and Sydney walked in together, Sandrine got up to greet them and saw their expressions. "*Uh-oh.*"

Teegan gazed at the newcomers and sighed. "So, now what?"

SANDRINE ASKED A bit awkwardly, "Do you want me to leave?"

Mountain nodded, while Sydney shook her head. He turned and glared at her, but she laughed. "We have to trust somebody. She's new here. She hasn't had anything to do with any of this mess, and she's also known Teegan for a while. I am very much in favor that she stays."

"I need to have confirmation first." He looked at Sandrine then and added, "I don't trust anybody around my brother right now, so … no offense intended."

"That's interesting." She frowned. "I do know a couple people who could vouch for me, but I doubt that you know them."

His eyebrows shot up. "Why is that?" he asked, a note of warning in his voice.

"Because most of the people I hung out with are in the medical field," she replied, with a shake of her head. Her eyebrows raised, and her jaw twitched. "I can't say one way or another if there would have been anybody you would know."

"And yet you knew my brother."

"Yes, and that's mostly because we went out for a while. As I was just telling him, when he asked me to marry him, he was stinking drunk, and I didn't take it seriously. He moments ago acknowledged it was probably not in the guidebook of how to get hitched."

Mountain's gaze shot from his brother back to Sandrine. "Do you remember meeting her?"

Teegan shook his head. "No, I don't remember much past waking up in the hole," he stated, "but I certainly recognized you. I would probably recognize a few other people, if I knew them before, but I can't guarantee that. So far, since waking up, I've only seen the three of you."

"And Amelia," Mountain noted. "You mentioned Amelia, even in the state you were in when I found you."

Teegan's face closed down, and he nodded. "And Amelia. You still haven't found her, have you?" he asked, his voice hard.

"No, I'm heading out now," Mountain announced. "It would help if you had some way to tell me where you were, how you lived, and what kind of surroundings you were in."

Teegan shook his head. "I can't tell you that," he snapped, his voice hard. "Believe me. If I could get up off this bed and head back out, with any expectation of finding her, I would already be gone."

"I get it," Mountain replied. "I do have some idea of where to look, … and I don't think she's too far away. The question is whether she's injured or in good shape."

"I don't know," Teegan admitted. "All I can tell you is that she's on the good side of life and that she's … terrified."

Mountain stepped forward, his gaze suddenly intense, and even Sydney looked at Teegan in shock. Doc asked him, "Terrified? Why? Of what?"

"She kept saying that we weren't safe and that she was doing what she could but it was getting to be too much."

Sydney stepped forward, until she stood right in front of

Teegan. "Did you ever see another person?"

He looked at her in surprise and then frowned. "A man," he replied, "but I don't know the circumstances."

Sydney nodded. "I was thinking that maybe Amelia had helped another man," she shared cautiously.

"Maybe, but, if that were the case, I don't know why she wouldn't be coming into the base. She ought to be safe here, right?"

"Yeah, that's been one of the questions we're all trying to sort out," Mountain replied. "There are questions though, and incidents that cause us to consider whether she's on drugs, was given drugs, or has had a lack of oxygen to the extent that she's quite compromised herself."

Sydney pitched in at this point. "It's also possible that she's either got delusions or paranoia or has come up with some concept of what's gone wrong within our military base. Therefore, she's been determined to keep you away from it."

"Either way," Mountain noted, "it's time that we find out if she's suffering from whatever condition you're talking about, where she thinks it's not safe to come back in again."

"I could buy that," Teegan shared. "I don't know about the rest of it."

"Don't worry. I'll track her down." Mountain stared at Teegan, then hesitated.

"Go," Teegan said. "I'm here. Sydney will look after me, and so will Sandrine. Nobody will get ... Nobody will touch me here, if that's what you're stressing over."

The way Teegan described it had Mountain sucking back his breath, and even Sandrine turned and looked at their patient. "You think you're still in danger?" she asked in a low voice.

He hesitated. "I don't know. ... I really don't know."

Mountain looked over at Sydney and stated, "I'm heading out now. You take care of them." He pointed to both of them, and, with that, he turned and quickly left the clinic.

Sandrine looked over at Sydney and wanted to ask if they needed security or if Teegan should be under guard, but Sandrine didn't know how to do that and not raise any panic in Teegan, if that should be the case. When a knock came on the clinic door, another man walked in, and she recognized Samson, the investigator.

"Hey," Sandrine greeted him, with half a smile. "Samson, I guess I should have expected to see you here."

He nodded. "I came to talk to Teegan." His gaze turned to Sydney, who frowned. Then Samson looked over at Teegan.

"I'm fine. I just don't have much in the way of answers."

"I get that," Samson noted, eyeing him closely. "First off, do you know who I am?"

Teegan shook his head. "Nope."

He nodded. "And, second, do you know who took you from here?"

"Nope, and, further to your question, … I'm not sure I was taken from here," Teegan clarified.

Sydney stepped forward and asked, "What do you mean?"

"I don't know, I'm not sure. I know another person was involved somehow. I thought I saw another person. I don't know whether that was another victim or …" He hesitated, frowning. "Maybe that was my kidnapper, if I even was kidnapped." He shook his head, as if to control the confusion rolling through his brain.

Samson nodded. "Got it. It seems as if you'll pull through this, but, obviously with the frostbite, you could have some issues. The supply plane has already left, and it'll return in two days. We hope to get you out of here then, weather permitting."

Sydney frowned. "What's up with that? I expressly asked them to delay their departure so we could get Teegan on the first plane heading stateside."

"There was a narrow window in the weather, so they took it in order to refill, refuel, and return again, as needed," Samson explained, speaking a bit sternly. "A destroyer is not too far away. If you deem it necessary to get Teegan shipped out immediately, let me know, and I'll see what I can do."

"You sure?" Sydney asked Samson. "The colonel won't be impressed with that, so I can't promise that we can make it happen."

"Oh, I can make it happen," Samson said.

He gave her a wry look, but it was so fleeting that Sandrine thought she must have imagined it.

Samson continued. "What I'm not sure about is whether it's necessary. The more people we have flying in and out of here, the harder it is to keep it all quiet."

"And why is it we're keeping it quiet?" Sandrine asked.

"Because we still don't know who attacked Teegan or who held him captive or if that person is related to this base," he shared. "Meanwhile everybody is currently on lockdown, including you, Sandrine, by the way," he stated, his gaze sharp. "You are instructed to stay here to assist in any way you can."

She stiffened slightly at that and then nodded. "Of course. That's what I came for anyway."

"And because you have only arrived, you'll have slightly more leeway but not a whole lot."

"Dogs," Teegan muttered out of the blue.

Samson stepped forward. "Dogs? What about them?"

"There were dogs," he repeated, and he seemed far away for a moment. Then he frowned. "But there are dogs here."

"Yes, there are dogs on base," Samson confirmed. "You were close with a couple, I understand."

Teegan smiled. "Kosta."

"Right. And Kosta is one that looks like Toby, who was shot," Samson noted, with an unfocused look around the room.

At that, Teegan lurched up in his hospital bed, and Sydney raced over, as Sandrine pressed him back down.

"You're not going anywhere," the doc said.

"Kosta was shot?" Teegan asked, staring at Samson in shock.

"No, Toby was, but he's alive."

"Jesus, who would hurt a dog?"

"Either somebody who missed his target and accidentally shot a dog or thought that shooting the dog would take that person out of commission," Samson suggested.

"Two dogs and Magnus were wounded in that incident," Sydney muttered.

"Ah." Teegan sighed, as he sank back. "We're back to the same damn bullshit then, aren't we?"

"If and when you get your memory back," Samson stated, straightening up, "we'll discuss the information you left behind."

He frowned at that. "Now if I only remembered what that information was."

"Exactly." Samson nodded, as he turned toward him. "We're currently going over everybody's statements from the beginning, yet again," he shared. "I'm coming in on the case and going through it with a fine-tooth comb to see what might have been missed."

"You're implying that something *was* missed though," Sydney pointed out, as she looked at him with a narrowed gaze. "I can tell you that every special investigator here has been working really hard to sort out this damn mess."

"I know," he replied, with a reassuring smile. "I've been getting reports on a regular basis, so I understand that."

She nodded, facing him squarely, then whispered, "I have an idea that I want to discuss with you outside." And, with that, she moved Samson into the hallway and closed the clinic door, leaving Sandrine and Teegan alone in the clinic.

She looked down at Teegan. "I don't know what that's all about, … but it seems Sydney has some sort of a plan."

"A plan is one thing," he replied, "but something that will get my memory back? That's a whole different story."

"It'll come," she declared. "Don't you worry. It'll happen."

He gave her a crooked smile. "How can you be so positive all the time? For all you know, your life could be in danger too." She stared at him in shock, and he shrugged. "It's one of the reasons I'm about to be sequestered with a guard," he noted, with a glance at the closed door. "When the shit hits the fan around this place, it really hits the fan."

TEEGAN DRIFTED IN and out of sleep for the rest of the day, and every time he woke up, he was looking for answers. By the time four o'clock rolled around, he was tired and frustrated. He noted Sandrine was not there, leaving the doc and Teegan alone in the clinic.

The doctor walked over and smiled down at him. "It

would be a lot easier if you wouldn't put so much pressure on yourself." He gave her a flat stare, and she chuckled. "And now you'll tell me that I'm off my rocker, and, of course, it doesn't matter."

"But it does matter," he stated. "Amelia, … she's still out there, and she's suffering."

Sydney nodded. "Can you tell me why she's suffering, in what way she's suffering, or something?" she asked, coaxing him. "Is she injured? Is she sick? Is she panicked? What is it?"

"I don't know. But every time I saw her, she was working hard to keep me alive, whether that was physically keeping me supplied or fighting people off."

"Did you see her fight anybody?" she asked sharply.

He nodded. "One time there was a confrontation, and I remember her yelling and arguing with somebody."

"Could you see anybody there?"

He frowned. "That's the thing. I couldn't see anything." She nodded, but he didn't like the expression on her face. "And now you're thinking she's crazy, I suppose."

"No, not at all," she corrected, studying him. "I'm just concerned that what we might take as being a fight is possibly—"

"You think she's hallucinating."

"It definitely happens," Sydney confirmed, "particularly if oxygen has been cut off for too long. It seems she's been out on her own, panicking and trying to hold it all together for a long time. That can play hard with your mental state."

"There's lots of oxygen," he snapped. Then he closed his eyes and reopened them, taking a deep breath. "I'm sorry. I'm not trying to be mean."

She laughed. "If that was being mean, it was a teddy-bear attempt." His eyes widened, and she nodded. "I've worked with a lot of men," she shared, "and I've worked with a lot of injured people. When things go ugly, they get ugly real fast and in a big way," she noted, with the wave of her hand.

He fidgeted, looking miserable and started to speak. "Look. I—"

"Don't apologize. You're worried about your friend, somebody you believe helped you and literally kept you alive. Nothing wrong in that."

"I just, … I want answers," he said in frustration. "I want to know what happened to me and who did this. And I hate to say it's even more important that I know why. I can't imagine what I could have possibly done to piss somebody off to this extent."

"Why do you think you pissed somebody off?"

He shrugged. "Can you imagine any other reason someone would do all this?"

"Yes, an awful lot of potential reasons. One, you were a stranger. Two, you were in the wrong place at the wrong time. Three, you overheard something you shouldn't have, so everybody thought you knew something you shouldn't. There are all kinds of reasons, whether you like it or not, that could have made you a target, without doing a thing," she explained, with a quick headshake. "Then there's the one where you simply fit a profile, … you fit somebody's profile."

"Are you saying you think a serial killer is on the loose in here?" he asked. "How could that be? This is a highly secure military operation."

"Army, navy, marines, and air force," she confirmed. "Keep that in mind. Plus they come from several different countries."

"But this is a friendly training center."

"I beg to differ."

"Meaning?"

"Meaning that somebody here isn't so friendly after all. Do you still consider it friendly after all that's happened to you?"

"No, of course not," he agreed, "but that doesn't mean what I worry happened to me is what really happened to me."

"Exactly. So, what we have to do is find out precisely what happened to you, so we have a much better idea and can prevent anybody else from being affected."

"God, yes," Teegan agreed. "The thought of anybody else going through what I did, … it's too much."

"Agreed. As it is, we've already had several deaths. You've been gone so long that I'm sure you haven't been informed about any of that," Sydney guessed.

Sandrine rejoined them, bringing hot coffee, and added, "Even though I am the newest one on base, I've heard all about the problems, the deaths, people murdered, gone missing, and potential suicides on the premises too."

He stared at Sandrine in shock.

Sydney nodded. "When things went wrong, they went wrong in a big way," she said, her voice calm. "So, it's not that nobody trusts you or believes you. It's just that there's been so much trouble already, all we can do is try to keep ahead of the game as much as we can and solve the problems as they come up."

"Jesus, that's unbelievable," Teegan muttered in shock.

"I know," she said, "and that's why we're all doing the best we can and trying to stay afloat. Nobody's expecting you to have answers any more than anyone else, but any information you do have will be golden for us because the investigators have had such a horrific time solving this," Sydney shared. "So, the more answers you can provide, the better chance we have of figuring it out and stopping whatever is happening, before anybody else gets hurt."

He nodded. "That makes sense. It's just so frustrating, since it appears that I can't even help, when I should be the one who does."

"Why?" the doc asked, staring at him. "Do you really think you'll be in a position to help more than anybody else?"

"No, not *more* than anybody else, but at least as much as anybody else."

"You're putting all that pressure on yourself, but, in the state that you're in, that's not helpful."

He groaned and settled back into the bed. "Maybe not, but sitting here, not able to do anything, isn't helpful either."

"Your first responsibility is to get well," she stated. "Anything else is secondary. Sandrine, why don't you take a break and get some sleep?" Sandrine nodded to the doc and smiled at Teegan, then left them again.

With that, the doc walked to her desk and sat down.

"Don't suppose I could have a laptop, *huh*?" He stared at Sydney, hopeful.

She considered it and then nodded. "For a little bit, if you want to check up on the world and get caught up on things going on in the news. I guess I don't have a problem with that." She brought over a laptop, turned it on, and put it beside him.

He frowned at it. "No power."

"Meaning?" she asked, stopping.

"At the snow cave, we didn't have power."

"No, I'm not surprised. If you think about it, wherever Amelia was keeping you, … wherever you were staying," she corrected herself, changing her tone, "I would have been surprised if it had any amenities."

"She kept trying to get me warm and kept telling me it was too dangerous to bring me back to base."

She sat down beside him. "Good, keep talking."

He winced. "I wish I could. … I wish I understood."

"Again, don't push it. Whatever comes up, comes up."

He nodded.

She got up and returned to her desk, where she sat down and, he presumed, continued to work on whatever it was she was dealing with.

He opened up the internet, only to realize that he couldn't access anything. "Do we have to sign in to the internet?" he asked, looking over at her. She nodded and got up, then logged in for him. "Thank you."

She shrugged. "Sorry, I should have done that to begin with. You might as well see what's happening in the world around you. It might jog something. Remember though, that satellite service here is spotty."

Teegan nodded and quickly hunted through the latest news to see what would pop up. Nothing was terribly good or bad about any of it, but is also wasn't helpful. Whatever was going on, he didn't have a clue, and no matter what he tried to do, it seemed as if he wasn't getting anywhere.

Despite the sickness in his soul, he checked the world news, checked anything local that he could find, and, when absolutely nothing else seemed to come up, he slowly closed the laptop. "I don't know what I thought I'd find."

"Answers," she stated. "We're always looking for answers."

"On the internet?" he asked, with a wry look.

"I'm sure you were looking wherever you thought you could find something," she said, "anything at all. Don't judge yourself for it. Just allow yourself to go with it. I would be interested to know what you searched for in terms of keywords."

"I typed in my name to search Google," he admitted, with a laugh, "to see if anybody had reported the fact that I was missing."

"Did you find anything?" she asked curiously.

"No, I gather I didn't make it to the news."

"You better not have," she noted, with a snort. "There would be hell to pay if you did."

"I guess. I hadn't thought of that."

"When there are problems on a military base, it's definitely not something you want the media to grab ahold of."

"No, but it would be nice to think that, if I had passed away, somebody, somewhere, would take notice."

"You really think your brother wouldn't?"

Startled, Teegan laughed. "One thing Mountain would have done is made sure the world had a good idea of what happened to me. That I can count on, always and forever."

"So, count on the fact that he's out there right now, busting his butt, trying to figure out what happened to you, so he can keep you safe from it happening again," Sydney stated. "You do your best to heal."

DAY 2 DINNERTIME

A T DINNERTIME, SANDRINE entered the dining room. She walked up to the buffet counter, looking to see how long it would be until food was put out. She still hadn't gotten into the routine of being here and hadn't really had a chance to even begin to fit in.

Several of the men stopped and frowned at her.

She smiled and nodded. "Yeah, hi, … medical relief."

"I thought nobody was coming in or out," one of the guys grumbled, with a shake of his head. "Seems as if a lot of people are coming in and going out, … but not us."

Another one of the group snorted, an unpleasant smile on his face.

Sandrine didn't say anything, but it was obvious to her that anybody who had been here through the whole nightmare wasn't allowed to leave, not until the brass got to the bottom of it, a plan she wholeheartedly agreed with. However, she could see that most of the guys here were not taking it very well. She shrugged. "Sorry, it is what it is," she said, as she moved into the kitchen.

Elijah stepped out then and looked at her curiously. "How's life?"

She laughed. "Life is fine," she murmured. "I'm not into the swing of things yet, so I wasn't sure when dinner was."

"You've got about twenty minutes yet."

"Good enough." She walked over to the hot water, where she quickly checked to see if it was actually hot.

Deciding it was hot enough for tea, she made herself a cup and slowly turned to head back down to the medical clinic. She didn't want to deal with people if they would be difficult, and neither did she want to deal with questions. So the best place for her right now would be in the clinic, along with Teegan. With that thought, she contemplated for a moment, then headed back over and poured another cup of herb tea.

She didn't know if he would want hot tea, but a hot drink might make all the difference. She could have brought him a coffee but wasn't sure that Sydney would allow it. The doc seemed to have pretty-strong feelings about what her patient was getting and what he wasn't.

As she got the second cup, one of the guys stepped up to her and looked at her rather unpleasantly.

"What's this? Two cups, *huh*?"

"Sure, why not?" she asked, with an offhand smile. "Don't have to come back quite so often."

"They'll both get cold."

"Maybe," she agreed, "and maybe they're for Sydney, the doctor."

He looked at her, a hard expression on his face, and she gave him a flat stare back. Working with guys like these for the last few years, Sandrine had learned something. She knew that giving in was the worst thing you could ever do in this situation. She didn't know anybody here, and her very arrival was apparently enough to earn the suspicious looks cast in her direction.

At that same moment, Elijah stepped up and barked at all of them. "What are you doing here already?" he yelled.

"Get out of my space, I'm trying to set up dinner. Go on, everyone. Get lost."

As she turned to go, Chef grabbed her arm and said sternly, "Not you."

She waited, and, as soon as the room cleared, he nodded with a careless wave. "Now you can go."

"Are they likely to hassle me?"

"I don't know what they'll do," he admitted. "In the past, I would have said *never*. But right now, things are pretty touchy."

A little more unnerved at the concept of *touchy* in a way she had never had to look at before, Sandrine nodded and headed straight to the medical clinic again. She walked into the room, and Sydney was treating several people here. Sandrine stopped and surveyed the space, noting that Teegan wasn't there. Frowning, she put down her two teas, wondering whether this was part and parcel of some grand plan or she had missed something. She quietly sat at her desk, ready to assist Sydney, as needed.

As soon as Sydney quickly worked through the group of people who had come to her clinic, she finally turned to Sandrine and nodded. "Glad you picked up on that."

"Yeah, I picked up on it, but where is he?" Sandrine asked. "I hate to not see him here."

"He's in the room next door, which is my quarters," Syndney explained. "Once I realized that I had several other people coming in, I didn't want Teegan here, since God knows it would only be an open invitation to speculation as to what was going on. Once it starts, then curiosity brings even more people in," she murmured.

At that, Sandrine nodded and pointed. "I brought some tea over for him."

"Good, take it to my room and give me a report on how he's doing."

With that, Sandrine grabbed the tea, walked out of the clinic and headed to the room next door. This time she didn't knock. She walked right in and found Teegan curled up on the bed, seemingly asleep.

She walked over and whispered, "Hey, you awake?" He opened his eyes and stared at her. She smiled. "I brought you some tea. Dinner's in about twenty minutes."

He nodded. "Elijah's really good," he muttered, his voice slurred with sleep.

Surprised that he even mentioned the chef by name, she nodded. "He is. Do you know him well?"

"Good guy. Always there for a conversation."

She stared at him, as he rolled over, groaned again at the pain as he shifted, but somehow managed to slip back under again. She sat down in the single chair and looked down at the tea, which she now had two solid cups of, and softly laughed. "I guess I'm having tea by myself then."

But just a few minutes later, Teegan woke up and shifted onto his back, gasping, but this time not crying out in pain or staring at her in surprise.

"Hey, I brought you tea, but it seems you are too sleepy."

He blinked at her several times and nodded. "Tea would be good." His voice was raspy.

She helped him shift into a sitting position, using pillows to prop him up.

"Why am I in here?" he asked, yawning. "I remember the doc moving me in here, but I don't know why."

"Because she runs an open clinic, and she only has two beds and some foldables in there," Sandrine explained. "She was afraid a bunch of looky-loos were coming to see who the new patient was."

"Ah, so secrecy on all counts."

"Are you against that?"

"No. That was quick thinking on her part. I am glad that she moved me here. Besides, I can't exactly answer any questions."

"And yet you just talked about Chef."

He frowned at her. "Did I say something about Elijah?" He shrugged. "I don't remember."

"You told me that he was a good guy and always easy to talk to."

"He is, and he's a good guy," Teegan confirmed. "So that's, … that's a decent analysis on my part, even if I wasn't really cognizant."

"I guess you probably had some interesting conversations with him over the time you were here."

"Probably. … I'm a friendly guy myself."

"I remember," she said, with a laugh.

He looked at her with a narrow gaze and then asked, "So, how close were we?"

"Close," she replied. "As I told you, you asked me to marry you."

"I remember you said that."

She snorted. "Believe me. I don't just say things."

"Good. … I wondered if we were, … if it was a bad breakup."

"No, not at all. You didn't take it as a rejection. You didn't say anything."

"Did you answer me though, or did you let me go off on my own, thinking that I was rejected, even though you hadn't come out and said so?"

She laughed. "I don't know if I did or not. I'm not sure you were aware enough to even hear me."

He winced. "God, I was that drunk, *huh?*"

"Yeah, you were definitely that drunk," she confirmed, with a snort.

"So, did we break up right afterward?"

"Pretty much," she said, with a nod. "You were heading out on a mission. And then, when you came back, you were posted to Germany."

"Oh, wow, and you stayed where?"

"I stayed in California."

"Okay, that tells me why we didn't work out."

"At the time it certainly didn't work," she quipped, with a cheeky look. "As a proposal, it certainly was one for the books."

He winced. "Sorry about that."

She burst out laughing. "God, don't be sorry. When you woke up, I got the impression that you were more embarrassed than anything."

"Oh, and that's even worse." He groaned. By now she was thoroughly enjoying herself. He glared at her. "It's hardly fair when I don't have any memories of it."

"No, that is quite true," she agreed. "On the other hand, you are certainly giving me something to chuckle about." His grin, when it came, was fast, furious, and slammed against her heart. "Wow. I think that is the first smile I've seen from you."

"Haven't had a whole lot to smile about," he pointed out.

"No, you sure haven't, but now you are safe, secure, and doing much better."

"Don't forget about hiding out in the doctor's bedroom," he added, with a smirk. "God, that's a weird thing to say."

"It doesn't matter," Sandrine stated firmly. "Doc's doing everything she can to keep you safe."

Teegan nodded. "I definitely got that impression, though I don't think she was so worried that something would happen as much as she was concerned that my presence would cause a lot of drama and uproar."

"I'm sure it would," Sandrine noted, with a nod, "and that would be something she would be right to avoid."

He didn't say anything for a long moment, and they sat there and sipped their tea. "Did I say anything else about Elijah?"

"That he was somebody you enjoyed having a conversation with—good for conversations. That was it."

He nodded. "Seems something else was there though."

"When you say, *something there*, what does that mean?"

"I'm not sure," he admitted, with a headshake. "I'm not sure. It's all, … all a big mess."

"Fine," she replied. He glared at her, and she nodded. "I know, Teegan. You're frustrated. You're angry, and you want answers, but more than that, you want your memories back. All I can tell you is that it'll take time."

He sank back and nodded. "I wish I didn't feel as if there wasn't time."

"Meaning?"

"Meaning, some sort of time element is involved."

"Outside of Amelia?"

He frowned at that and then nodded. "Yeah, outside of Amelia, there's some time element. I don't know what it means."

AS FAR AS Teegan hoping a conversation with Sandrine would jog something in his head, all it did was piss him off and make him angry. He couldn't blame Sandrine for it. Hell, he didn't have even a hint of recognition of her, though surprisingly he felt a sense of familiarity, as if he did, indeed, know her. The most awkward thing was that he hadn't had that same feeling with anybody else, except for his brother.

As soon as Teegan had seen Mountain, something had slammed home into his brain, and he'd known exactly who he was. Maybe because he'd been so desperately calling out for Mountain the whole time he had been gone. Desperate for answers, desperate for help, desperate for somebody to figure out that he was missing and where he was.

After checking on Google for the current date, Teegan had done some basic calculations, realizing with shock how long he'd been missing. And how long somebody had been screwing around with his life. That had shocked him more than anything else. When Sydney had taken the laptop away from him, he hadn't protested because it seemed so far-fetched to even sit here in that stupor and not have answers. That part was driving him crazy. And it wasn't fair because he had done so much work this entire time, trying to do whatever he was doing up here, regarding the survival training.

Then a name popped into his head, and he said it out loud. "Mason."

Sandrine looked over at him, obviously not hearing him clearly. "What did you say?"

"Mason."

"What about Mason?"

Teegan shrugged. "I don't know. His name came up."

"Okay. Is it somebody we need to contact? Is it somebody who would be missing you? Is it …" She frowned, then added in a lower voice, "I've heard of Mason, but I don't personally know him."

He shrugged. "I'm not sure I do either. Just a name that came up."

A few minutes later, while they were still tossing the name back and forth, the door opened. and Sydney walked in. She smiled and said, "So much for coming back and giving me a report."

With astonishment, Sandrine's face turned bright red, and she jumped to her feet. "Oh my gosh, I'm so sorry. I knew you were busy in there with other people, and I held off at first, thinking that because you had no problem you wouldn't need me to come in and report, but obviously I should have told you that right away."

"No, it's fine, and you're right. I didn't expect there to be a problem, and obviously you're both fine," the doc noted, with a steady gaze in his direction. "It's okay, but, in the future, if I ask for a report, I expect to get one."

Sandrine nodded, her face changing color in embarrassment.

Teegan almost felt sorry for her and tried to lighten up the conversation. "The good news is, I'm sitting here, having tea." He sounded as if he were in a good mood. "I was sleeping heavily, and your bed's very comfortable, by the way. I feel bad that I'm here."

The doc shook her head. "I would feel much worse if you weren't sleeping." She sent him a smile. "So, we'll call it good, and you can come back over to the clinic, if you want." With that, she helped Teegan to his feet and assessed his ability to walk.

"Can I go to the bathroom first?" he asked.

"Yeah, since I took out the catheter earlier, you sure can."

He winced. "Yeah, thanks for that reminder."

She chuckled. "Hey, it's the easiest way to deal with unconscious patients. We have limited resources here," she shared, "so I'm really not too bothered about the sense of personal space. I'm more concerned about the fact that you haven't used the bathroom since."

"I did," he confessed. "I snuck out after you sent me to your room." She stared at him in astonishment. He shrugged. "I couldn't go back in and say something to you when it was obvious you didn't want me in there," he explained. "So, I made my way down the hallway. It's not very far away."

"No, it's not," she agreed, yet with a stern glance. "Yet I would have preferred that you hadn't gone on your own, but that's on me," she admitted.

"It's probably on me," Sandrine added. "I think you wanted me back to look after him, and I was a little bit late getting here."

"I'm fine," Teegan said to both women. "Come on, people. I went to the bathroom. That's it."

"I know, and you could have collapsed," Sydney pointed out in a gentle voice. "The fact that you didn't is huge."

"Great. Honestly, I shouldn't need a babysitter, certainly not like this," he muttered.

"No, I get that," Sydney said, with a chuckle. "But remember? We're not giving everybody notice that you're here—not yet."

"Yeah, well, you say that, but, in this base or any military base, believe me. News travels faster than the speed of light."

"Oh, gosh," Sandrine agreed. "He's right, and I got asked about the extra cup of tea when I brought it back for him. I'm sorry. I wasn't thinking that I was supposed to hide it. I did tell them it was for you, though."

"It doesn't matter that much," Sydney replied, "but trying to keep something quiet is different from telling people that he's here."

"Yet I'm sure people know that he's been found, don't they?" Sandrine asked. "How could they not?"

"I'm assuming so, but that doesn't mean I have any authorization to tell people," Sydney clarified. "So keeping things quiet for now is just easier. I'm waiting for Mountain to return. Then he can make any announcements, as he sees fit."

"Oh, that makes sense," Sandrine replied.

"Speaking of Mountain, where is my brother?" Teegan asked.

The doc turned to him. "He hasn't come back yet." Teegan sucked in his breath. Sydney shook her head. "Of all the things that we've learned, when it comes to your brother, he's a law unto himself here, and, when it comes to these trips, he comes and goes unnoticed and unceremoniously."

Teegan glared at Sydney, and Sandrine smiled at him. "As you well know, he's perfectly capable of looking after himself out there."

"Yeah, and what else I know," he snapped, "is that I would have said the exact same thing about me, and look where I ended up."

Sydney glared at him. "I won't worry about Mountain

for now," the doc said in a strict tone. "You're my patient, so you're the one I'm looking after. Mountain's a grown-ass man, and I certainly won't worry about where he is right now. He comes and goes like a ghost, and I frankly don't have the energy."

At that, a knock came on her door. Magnus poked his head around the frame and shared, "Wow, your bedroom got cozy."

"Yeah, it did." The doc turned to Magnus. "Could I ask you to take Teegan to the men's room, making sure that it's empty first," she requested, her tone flat, "then bring him back to the clinic." And, with that, she stepped out of her bedroom.

Teegan looked from one to the other. "I don't know if I said something wrong," he began apologetically, "but I really could use a trip to the bathroom. Plus apparently, the doc wants me out of her space. So anytime you feel like it, I am beyond ready."

"It is her bedroom," Magnus noted. "Let's get you down to the bathroom and back into the medical clinic. She hasn't had a break in quite a while, and it's been pretty intense up here for even longer," he shared.

Teegan understood the undercurrents between Magnus and the doc. "So, am I wrong in assuming this is also your room?"

He gave Teegan half a smile. "Officially there are no co-ed rooms up here, as you well know but may have forgotten. However, if you're asking if the two of us are in a relationship, then the answer is yes."

"Lucky you," Teegan muttered. "On the other hand, after what she did to me with that catheter, she's all yours, dude."

His laughter rolled out rich, and, smiling ear to ear, Magnus replied, "Not a problem. I can handle her just fine." He looked over at Sandrine and suggested, "You can head over to the clinic."

She hopped to her feet, grabbed the cups, and headed to the clinic, as Teegan looked back at Magnus.

"It's Magnus, isn't it?" Teegan asked him.

"It is. Do you remember me?"

"No, I don't think so." Teegan frowned.

"Good. If you would have said yes, I would have called you a liar. The fact that you answered truthfully means that I can trust what you say."

"What do you mean?"

"I came after you'd disappeared," Magnus began. "I was part of a team who came to find you."

"Thank God for that. You have my gratitude."

"Gratitude is one thing," he replied, with a nod, "but finding out what the hell's going wrong with this place? That's a whole different story. Believe me. Now that we've got you, Mountain is all over it."

"He might be," Teegan acknowledged, "but I also insisted that he look for Amelia. He needs to find her."

"He's been looking for Amelia all along too. I don't know if he found her and left her be or what, but, if that's the case, then I'm sure he's kicking himself for not finding you up until now."

"I don't know anything about that," Teegan noted, his voice low. "I just know that everybody here will think the worst of her, and they shouldn't."

"If she has done nothing wrong, they won't." Magnus pointed at the wall. "Stay here."

Teegan leaned back gently and waited while Magnus

quickly went out, maybe to check the restroom first. He came back moments later, affirming that the course was clear. They slowly walked to the bathroom, where Teegan quickly used the facilities, trying to ignore the face in the mirror.

"Even if somebody did see me here, someone who knew me from before, they sure as hell wouldn't recognize me."

"That's a good point," Magnus agreed cheerfully, "but, if we could stop anybody from even seeing you, that would be better."

"It's that bad, *huh*?"

"It's that bad," he confirmed. "It's all secrets right now because somebody here is responsible for all this shit," he declared. "And believe me. Nobody is looking to let anybody out of here until it's solved. So now that you're back in the land of the living, everybody'll be turning to you for answers."

"What if I don't have any?" he asked, staring at Magnus.

Magnus laughed. "Given enough time, I sure as hell hope you do. We've had way too many people get hurt, and all this needs to stop."

And, with that, he led Teegan right back to the medical clinic and firmly locked the door, keeping him inside.

DAY 3 MORNING

THE NEXT DAY Sandrine was kept busy with a steady stream of visitors to the medical clinic. As soon as one person got sick, the virus spread rapidly throughout the base. She cast a glance over at the bed they had screened off with a series of sheets, so Teegan could stay here and didn't have to keep moving back to Sydney's room.

All trainings had been suspended in order to curtail the spread of the virus. Even as Sydney worked tirelessly beside Sandrine, the two women looked at each other several times. By lunchtime they had treated well over a dozen.

"Wow, this is not a good scenario," Sandrine noted.

Sydney laughed. "No, it sure isn't," she muttered. "On the other hand, the sooner that they're over it, the better."

"But how do we stop them from spreading it to other people?" Sandrine asked her boss. "It seems nobody is too bothered about keeping their distance or avoiding close contact with the others."

"That's because everybody is so fed up with staying bundled up inside," the doc shared, with a shrug. "Giving orders to stay in bed is the best I can do right now, and they will stay in bed because otherwise I'll have guards posted," she explained. "Still, it won't change anything. In the end, this virus will just run its course." Shaking her head, Sydney added, "Chances are, everybody's already infected at this point anyway, and the best we can do is try to keep it under control somewhat."

"Great," Sandrine muttered. "*Somewhat* doesn't exactly sound all that inspiring for me or anyone else here for that matter."

The doc laughed. "No, I don't guess it would." She smiled. "On the other hand, we've had viruses, colds, and flus hit other bases. This isn't life-threatening by any means. It's just an inconvenience, and people need to smarten up and to look after themselves,"

"But, with everybody as uptight and irate and stressed as they are, it becomes a bigger deal," Sandrine pointed out, with a roll of her eyes.

"Exactly. The fact is, everybody's immune system has taken a hit, and even the stress alone will do that. Our job is to keep everybody as healthy as possible, which we're not doing very well at all right now," she said in frustration. "However, in the end, not a whole lot we can do," she noted. "Everybody just needs to relax and to let this virus work its way through. Meanwhile we also must ensure that we don't drop in the process."

"Exactly. What about Teegan?" Sandrine glanced at his screened-off bed.

"I'm here, in case you're wondering," Teegan replied, from the other side of the curtain. "Don't mind me, while you are dilly-dallying over there."

"I won't," Sandrine called out, with a laughing voice. "Particularly if I know that you're lying there and listening. That's good enough, if you're not moving a muscle."

"I'm hardly listening to anything secret," he noted, "particularly when I don't have any choice and when you're talking right there."

Sandrine walked over, slightly pulled back the curtain, and stepped into his little makeshift privacy booth. "How're you feeling?"

He stared at her and replied in a sarcastic tone, "How do you think I'm feeling?"

"Caged," she said. "I know I would."

He nodded. "I'm starting to feel well enough that I want out of here, but not well enough that I can make that happen," he shared, with a sigh. "As soon as I start to feel better and to get all cocky, thinking I'm fine, … everything blows up," he admitted. "I went to the bathroom and felt decent, then came back, shaking and with chills."

Sandrine nodded. "And I can't imagine that'll stop anytime soon. We're doing everything we can for you, but …"

"I know. I know," he muttered, as he shifted under the covers, as if still looking for warmth.

She smiled. "You're handling it very well."

"Oh, yeah, sure," he quipped. "Now you're trying to butter me up."

She chuckled. "It's not working though, is it?"

"No, unfortunately," he said, propping himself up. "It would be nice if it did, though." He settled back on the bed and noted, "If you guys aren't using the laptop, I could use one. Or, for that matter, I would love to know what happened to mine."

"Did you have one?" Sandrine asked.

He frowned at her but nodded. "I think so."

She pursed her lips. "Maybe we should ask your brother for it then."

"Sure, as long as *you* ask him," he stated, a big grin on his face. "He's a bit touchy right now."

She groaned. "Knowing me, I would probably say the

wrong thing."

He shook his head. "At this point, I'm sure it's already the gossip everybody's heard."

"Maybe, but, until I've been given the word, I can't do anything about that."

"Nope, and my brother's not very good at opening up," Teegan pointed out in a frustrated tone, "so this will stay as quiet as he can make it."

"I'm not against that," Sandrine clarified. "It sounds as if enough has been going on here that I think we should all be very grateful that Mountain is keeping it as quiet as he can."

"Maybe. However, it would be awfully nice to have this out in the open, so I could wander around and maybe hit the dining room, without alarming everyone in the place."

She asked him, "Are you hungry?"

"No, not hungry," he said, "bored."

She frowned at him. "You can stop being bored." He stared at her in astonishment, and then she laughed. "Right. Not quite so easy at that," she acknowledged, with a chuckle. "We've been kind of busy on this end, in case you haven't noticed. And, with everybody getting sick, the last thing we need is for you to catch the bug flying around here. Your immune system can only take so much, you know?"

He shrugged but settled deeper into his blankets. "Just the thought of it gives me the shakes again," he admitted. "That's what I mean. I think I'm doing fine. Then, all of a sudden, I'm not doing fine at all. I am tired of this BS."

"I'm heading down to get a cup of coffee," Sandrine announced. "Would you like one?"

Clearly pleased, he smiled. "Thank you. I would love one."

She quickly walked out of the room, leaving Sydney

holding down the fort, as Sandrine headed to the dining room. There, tired and desperately needing some mental reinforcements of her own, she grabbed three coffees, then realized she should only take two, in order to make it look as only the two of them were in the clinic. She also picked up a few cinnamon buns, sitting off to the side, then headed back to the clinic.

Several people saw her come and go, but nobody mentioned anything, and that was good. As soon as she was back inside the clinic, she looked over at Sydney. "The problem with trying to keep Teegan a secret," she grumbled, "is I can only carry two servings at a time."

Sydney laughed, giving her a reassuring smile. "That's all right. I'm heading into a meeting anyway, so I can do without until I come back."

"Are you sure?" Sandrine asked, looking down at the tray. "I can probably slip back in and get another without anybody noticing."

"No, don't do that," Sydney replied. "This is probably the best answer anyway. I'll need you to hold down the fort while I'm gone." With that, she grabbed her notebook and went to open the door.

"I didn't even know you had a meeting."

"Neither did I, until now," the doc said, with an eyeroll. And, with that, she quickly hurried out of the clinic, leaving Sandrine alone with Teegan.

She walked into the little sectioned-off area, where Teegan was. As she pulled back the curtain, he slowly rolled over and looked at her, smiling. "I'm awake."

"Just checking," she said in a gentle voice. She retrieved the tray and brought in his coffee and a cinnamon bun.

His face lit up when he saw the treat. "Okay, that'll

help," he murmured.

She chuckled. "I've never quite understood that myself, but it absolutely does help improve moods, doesn't it?"

"You mean treats? Hell, yes." Teegan nodded. "It absolutely does. And God knows that anything to improve the mood in this place is invaluable."

She handed him the tray and helped him to sit up in a different position, trying not to disturb all his scabs and blisters and open wounds. She checked out his face and how much fatigue was revealed there, seeing how he was handling life today.

"I'm fine," he said, not even looking at her. "Every time you come in here, you're checking me out."

She snorted. "You make that sound so not what it is."

He looked over at her, grinned, and stated, "Maybe it should be."

"Oh, no, I went there one time," she replied cheerfully. "Can't say that's on my list again."

He stared at her, then slowly nodded. "No, I guess not, *huh*? Sorry. I didn't mean to hurt you, if I did."

"Of course not," she studied him. "Asking me to marry you was quite a compliment, but not necessarily a compliment that I would chose to hear again under those circumstances."

"Right. So, it was okay to think about, but not necessarily an okay idea."

"If you'd been serious, I might have thought about it," she replied in a careful tone. "Honestly, I thought we were pretty good together."

"And yet you didn't say yes."

"And yet you didn't repeat the offer when you were sober," she pointed out.

He winced. "Yeah, there's that, isn't there?"

"You probably scared yourself silly," she suggested, with a smile.

"I wouldn't be at all surprised," he admitted, now laughing. "It seems like a long time ago, and I still can't remember most of it."

"That's understandable, considering everything you've been through. And if you've remember any of it, that's progress."

He looked at her and nodded. "I was thinking about that. Any chance I could get a pad of paper and a pen?"

"Sure, I can manage that. Are memories coming back?"

"I want to try to bring some up. Bits and pieces are waffling through my head, yet nothing I can work with," he shared. "It's really frustrating, but I want to keep a record, even if it's just disjointed bits and pieces."

"Sure, give me a minute."

She walked back to the desk, found a pad of paper from Sydney's collection, grabbed a pen from the drawer, and brought it back. "Here you go. See what you can come up with," she suggested, putting it down in front of him. "I know an awful lot of people hope you can come up with something."

"Right? But no pressure," he teased, with an eyeroll. "That's always the worst."

"Pressure is mostly what you put on yourself. Everybody wants answers, but you can't give what you don't have, right? Don't stress yourself out about it."

"How do you *not* stress yourself out, when you know that somebody did this to you and how that same person could be here on the base right now?"

She stared at him, then looked back at the clinic door

and nodded. "That gives me a creepy feeling."

"And it should," Teegan confirmed. "For all I know, I'm putting you in danger by being here."

"Okay, I won't even think about that," she declared, raising both hands. "So, don't go there. Not now."

"Sticking your head in the sand won't work long-term," he pointed out.

"It might," she quipped. "It'll certainly work long enough for me to get through my day," she pointed out, "and right now it's just me here."

Then came a knock on the door. She quickly closed up the curtain and headed out to deal with whoever had arrived. Turned out, it was Magnus.

He asked, "Sydney's not here?"

"No, she got called to a meeting," Sandrine replied, then watched as an odd look crossed his face. "She didn't look too thrilled about it either."

"No, I'm sure she isn't. A lot of sick people are here right now, and I'm sure everybody is trying to figure out what she can do about it."

"As you likely already know, it's a virus," Sandrine explained. "Not a whole lot anybody can do about it. This is a medical clinic in a training base. It's not as if we have some shocking new treatments to cure them instantly. And I get it. Everybody wants an instant treatment. Everybody wants to feel better, but ..." Then she shrugged. "Hey, I don't know. Maybe Sydney's got some magical, mystical answers that I don't know about, but if she does, ... I haven't seen them work yet."

He laughed. "No, common colds and flus are one thing, and trying to keep people safe while they're busy spreading the germs left and right so openly in their spare time is a whole different story."

She winced at that. "Yeah, not exactly everybody's cup of tea, but you won't stop people from being people."

"And right now, nobody really wants to be alone, and yet they aren't that happy to be together either," he pointed out. "More fear is going on around here than anything."

"Which is not easy to deal with," Sandrine admitted, then motioned at the curtain. "Teegan pointed out that he could be putting me in danger, just by being here."

Magnus frowned. "Thanks for that, Teegan."

"I KNOW, RIGHT? Yet I'm not a fool," Teegan replied, from behind the curtain, as Magnus moved in to face him. "Something clearly happened to me already, so what's to say somebody won't make a second visit?"

"Which is why we've already been discussing security for you."

"Does everybody know already?"

"No, but there are plenty of rumors. We were waiting for somebody to make a formal announcement, but, so far, the colonel is committed to keeping a lid on your return."

"Right. But then I haven't heard a whole lot of good about our beloved colonel since I came up here, unless I forgot that too." Teegan's tone was laced with sarcasm. The fact that he had a feeling of animosity based on the competence of the colonel surprised him a bit, but it must have come from somewhere.

"He's in his own battle and is taking this assignment as a kind of punishment. He's putting in the time, so he can get his pension and get out … soon," Magnus explained. "And considering all the shit that's been going on, it does make you wonder if somebody isn't trying to prevent him from getting that last check. Or set him up to an ignoble end of forced retirement."

They talked for a few more minutes, and then Magnus quickly left. As soon as he was gone, Sandrine walked over, closed the clinic door, and then returned to Teegan. "Did you hear what Magnus said?" she asked Teegan.

"It was an odd thing for him to say."

"What? You mean about the colonel? It's kind of the reality, when you get somebody like that in charge. He figures he can run this place with his hands behind his back. He doesn't particularly care about the outcome, such as who survives, or who doesn't, and absolutely nothing any of us can do about it. The colonel just wants clear of this place, this mission, and likely his career. But no one wants to go out in disgrace. How much was under his control? Still, the buck stops with him."

"But that's just wrong," she muttered, staring at Teegan. "Just plain wrong."

He nodded. "Poor leadership has been the cause of many a military death," Teegan noted. "And I'm not saying he's doing anything wrong, but we all know that he's putting in his time and wants a peaceful exit."

"And yet it's not happening," Sandrine noted forcefully. "Nothing peaceful about this. People have been dying in this base for far too long."

"And yet, how many people are dying?" Teegan asked pointedly. "I'm here. It's not as if I died."

"No," she replied cautiously, thinking about it, "but we did have several people die within these walls."

"That may be, but was that because of the colonel? Because of this training base? Because of the scientists' camp?"

She winced and nodded. "Fine. My understanding is that two died here from the scientists' camp, plus Amelia is also from that place. All of their other colleagues either got out of here or left on their own. It sounded as if some fled the scene, but I still think something is seriously wrong with this base. Too many people have gone missing, and the accidental deaths are off the charts. Not to mention two murders—Helsky and Carl, right under the nose of our investigative team—so something is rotten at the core here."

"Oh, I agree with you," Teegan replied, "100 percent, but that doesn't change the fact that, until we know and can find out if anyone here is doing this, we don't know the extent of what they're doing and who is actually doing it. And that means we can't blame poor leadership—although the colonel will get full blame."

"Are you sure?" she asked, with a smirk. "I think anybody who is guilty of all this would like that."

"Maybe so." Teegan nodded. "The brass always makes a great scapegoat," he noted. "Doesn't mean it's always deserved though."

And, with that, she heard another knock on the door and whispered to Teegan to shut up. "Duty calls." And, with that, she quickly escaped and handled the next patient. It would obviously be a busy day, and that was putting it mildly.

Sure enough, the pace didn't let up, so Teegan was stuck behind the curtain all day.

With the pad of paper in his hand, off and on throughout the afternoon he napped, took notes, and then napped some more. Every time he came out of a dream, he seemed to force a little bit more information from his memory banks.

By the time Magnus returned to check up on him several hours later, he found Teegan dozing, with the pad of paper in his hand. Magnus took the notepad from his hand to set it on the side table, when Teegan opened his eyes, startled at the touch.

"Jesus, you scared me."

Magnus looked at the paper, reassuringly patting the hand that had gripped the pad, and looked at him. "Anything?"

"Bits and pieces," Teegan said. "Not sure any of it's helpful though. Little tidbits that don't fit anywhere."

"Such as?"

"The name Mason. Remembering bits of my history with Sandrine. Seeing somebody at the generator room, who wasn't expected to be there," Teegan began. "Yet, if you ask me who it was, I can't tell you. All I can see is the outfit. It's the same damn parka we all were issued here," he shared. "So, it could be just about anybody."

"Did you ever meet anyone in the local village?" he asked.

Teegan frowned at him and then slowly nodded. "Yes, I did."

"Did you ever wonder if anybody there could be involved somehow?"

"Why would they be?" he asked, and then he frowned and shrugged. "And I can't say if they were or not. I don't have any recollection of that. Obviously, if they had an agenda against us, then maybe," he suggested, "but I certainly didn't see anything along that line."

Magnus nodded. "What about Amelia? Do you remember seeing her at any other time prior to this?"

"No." And then he frowned. "No, I don't think so."

"So, she introduced herself to you?"

He looked up at him and shrugged. "I guess." But he was hesitant. "You're asking a question that I can't answer."

"All I'm doing is asking questions," Magnus stated. "I'm not looking for you to come up with answers. I'm only looking for you to tell me if you *do* have an answer."

"And you think there's a difference?"

Magnus nodded. "Absolutely." He gave him a half smile. "It's not a test, and I'm not asking for answers you don't have, but obviously we have some issues going on here that we could really use some help with."

"Not to mention my own safety," Teegan added, with a hard look. "I want to get up and out of here, but they want to keep me here, until the announcement's been made."

"Absolutely. I don't think there's any doubt who you are though, and, as much as we might be trying to keep it quiet, there's no keeping something like that 100 percent quiet in this base."

"I know. Sandrine went to get us all some coffee, but somebody had to do without because three cups would have been too many cups."

"And yet anybody would have or could have surmised it might have been some kind of a treat," Magnus suggested, with a shrug.

"It's a constant issue though. People have been coming in the clinic all day. They recognize somebody's back here, but nobody's willing to say anything, so that just adds to the mystery. Any idea when they'll announce it?"

"Today, I assume," Magnus noted. "I don't know when, and, then again, it depends on the colonel and whether he wants to announce it at all."

"So that'll add to it as well." Teegan groaned.

"It doesn't matter what it adds to. We just need to ensure that, whenever that announcement gets made, somebody is watching everybody in the crowd."

"Right, to see any reaction or anybody causing any issue."

"Exactly. We don't know if anybody here had something to do with all this chaos, but I don't understand how it couldn't be to some degree," Magnus acknowledged. "Of course that means everybody is looking at everybody sideways."

"Yeah, sorry about that," Teegan muttered. "I can't even guarantee that it was somebody here."

"According to Joe, you would spend time with the dogs, and, with some of your spare time, or under the guise of doing some sort of reconnaissance work, you would take a team and head out."

He looked over at him. "I would. Kosta." He grinned as the memory of the Inuit dog filled his memories. "I had a special preference for Kosta."

"Kosta is one of many."

"Absolutely. I didn't mean to say that only Kosta was any good, but, if I could take Kosta, I would."

"I'm wondering if that's why Toby got shot. He and Kosta look very similar. Both with distinctive black shoulders. If the dogs were used to identify the skier, then it would make sense."

"But I was already missing by then, wasn't I?"

"Yes, but what if you had gone missing from whoever had you? Amelia rescued you from someone, so maybe that person came back and shot Toby, confusing him for Kosta. Amelia may have had reservations, and that's why she didn't bring you back in to the base, just to protect you from the enemy within these walls."

Teegan stared at him for a long, hard moment. "So, you're thinking that Amelia saved me, but then, not knowing whom to trust, decided to keep me out there with her."

"I'm inclined to support that theory, but, in some ways, I don't know that it really fits either," he admitted. "I hate to think that she's responsible for your being out there all that time, but, at the moment, we're all confused. She may be the only one with answers to all this."

Teegan pondered that throughout the afternoon, and, when Sydney stepped in behind the curtain and checked on him before dinnertime, he said, "I hear there'll be an announcement today."

"There is, indeed," she confirmed. "You should be in much better shape to go out and handle whatever comments come your way."

"Will I be released into the public space?" he asked.

"You'll get your own room back and be released to roam the place freely—or maybe with some protection, as they see fit," she shared. "I'll take you, if you're capable, down for dinner tonight, and you will have one of us with you at all times when you're out on the base. Let's wait until they make the announcement though."

"So, in other words, I'll be under guard," he mumbled, closing his eyes and frowning. "All the damn time?"

"You got a better way to do it?" a man asked, his hard voice coming from the doorway.

He opened his eyes to see his brother and couldn't stop the wave of relief at the realization that he was back, safe and reasonably sound. "Hey. Glad to see you're back."

Mountain nodded and studied him. "You look better,"

he replied, with a pleased note in his voice.

"Yeah? I feel better. Not, … not a whole lot better yet."

"I got it." Mountain smiled. "But we'll take it, … one step at a time. You're alive. That's what counts."

"Agreed." He picked up the pad of paper and waved it around. "I've been sitting here this afternoon, trying to put down anything helpful. Trouble is, so many gaps are in my memory right now that I'm not sure anything is all that helpful."

"There's helpful, and then there's helpful," Mountain replied cheerfully. "We'll take pretty much anything at this point."

"Did you find Amelia?"

"No, I sure didn't. I did talk to the villagers though, and, under pressure, they conceded that she was incredibly popular and has come year after year and has made a lot of friends among the community. So, nobody is too willing to help me find her."

At that, Teegan nodded. "I can't see that she's behind any of this."

"Maybe not," Mountain conceded, "but I need more than that to go on."

"Of course you do." Teegan smiled. "Not like you to trust her on nothing but words."

"Would you?" Mountain asked, a note of challenge in his voice. "Whatever you didn't trust about all this before you went missing is what got you into this shit," he declared, with a hard voice. "All I'm trying to do is figure out who's on the other side of it. You get kidnapped. You have no idea how, where, or why. You're held for all that time. Then, all of a sudden, out of the blue, you're returned. I still don't understand quite how and why any of it happened."

"I don't know either," Teegan admitted, "but I don't want you barking up the wrong tree. I don't want you thinking that Amelia is behind this."

Mountain replied, "I don't have any choice *but* to think that." His tone was harsh. "And as long as she remains out there, lurking in the shadows and unwilling to come in and talk to me, she remains a person of interest."

Teegan laughed. "In your world, everybody's a person of interest."

That coaxed a grudging smile out of Mountain. He walked over and grabbed Teegan's shoulder and squeezed it gently. "Regardless, I'm damn glad to have you back."

"And that's another reason why I don't want you to go tearing her apart and accusing Amelia of anything," he pointed out. "She's good people."

"I'm glad to hear that," Mountain replied, "but, until the day that good people step up and talk to me, … I won't believe you."

Teegan snorted. "You don't believe anybody anyway, so that's nothing new." When Mountain glared at him, Teegan nodded. "It's true."

"I don't know how true it is," Mountain countered, "but what I will tell you is that we must have answers. That's the only way this base will get out from under its own shadow."

"And is that important?" Teegan asked. "Most of us will head off to our own world, one way or another," he pointed out, "and nobody'll really remember this as anything but the base from hell. Our CO gets to retire. He gets his fat pension, and the rest of the world carries on." Teegan shrugged. "I don't think anything here will make much of a difference either way."

"I'm not so sure about that," Mountain disagreed.

"Honestly, it's taken a bit, but definitely a few puzzle pieces are coming together." He eyed his brother. "Now that I've got you back, safe and sound, I need the rest of the missing pieces. At present, the next logical piece of this jigsaw puzzle is Amelia."

Teegan snapped, "She's not the missing piece. She's as much of a victim in all this as everybody else."

Mountain's eyebrows shot up. "How do you figure?" he asked.

"I don't know," he admitted, shaking his head, "but I can tell you, she's not on the bad-guy side. Either she's still trying to avoid capture herself or something else is going on, but I know for a fact that she was terrified for my sake and for her own."

"In that case, it's even more important that she come in," Mountain stated. "At least then we have a chance of keeping her safe."

At that, Teegan shook his head. "I don't think so. … I'm pretty sure she thinks the danger is in here."

"And again, if she doesn't say anything, we have no way to know what that danger is and how to stop it. And does she have any firsthand knowledge of it? That's the main question."

"I think she does," Teegan suggested, "because I can tell you one thing I do know. You may not want to believe me, but she was terrified. Over and over she kept telling me to live, that I needed to live, that the bastard couldn't win."

Mountain stepped forward and asked, "Did she say anything else about that bastard?"

"No, not at all, just that the bastard couldn't win." Teegan handed over the few notes he'd made. "And honestly, this is all that came up through my dead brain today."

"The fact that anything came up," Sydney replied, from behind Mountain, "is amazing. You need to take it easy and stop trying to force this. … The memories will come back easier that way."

"Maybe, but I don't know if they'll come back in time to save Amelia."

"Do you really think saving her is part of the issue?" Mountain asked.

"Absolutely, without a doubt," Teegan declared. "I don't know who's trying to stop us from saving her, but I bet you somebody out there doesn't want her to tell you what's going on. I want you to find her before this asshole gets her."

Mountain turned his attention to the notepad and sifted through the scarce information. "Amelia is one issue," he stated, "but right now the bigger question is you and what you need to return to health and to get your memory back, so we can figure out who is causing all this."

"I can't tell you who is doing this." Teegan sighed. "I am getting bits and pieces back but nothing truly helpful."

"Did Amelia mention dogs? Did she mention weapons? Did she mention leadership? Did she mention a name or a location?"

Teegan sagged back against the bed. "Do you really think I haven't been sitting here and racking my brain for all of those answers?" he cried out. "She had dogs sometimes though. I remember them lying close all the time and me burrowing in deep for their warmth."

"Of course you have," Mountain replied in a soothing voice. "But that doesn't mean you'll have any answers coming through right away. Just be open to it and understand that saying the names and all of it coming up in conversation can have a triggering effect. Think nothing of it and try to get some rest when you can. Look. I'm heading down to the dining room, and I'll bring you back some dinner."

"I thought there would be an announcement tonight?"

"There is," Mountain confirmed, "but I don't know when. I was hoping it would be at dinnertime."

"If it'll be at dinnertime, how about letting me come? Let me be there, so I can see the reaction on everybody's faces."

Mountain hesitated and looked over at Sydney.

The doc shrugged. "It's not a bad idea, and, if nothing else, it might help us to sort out what's going on here."

"It won't help anything," Mountain snapped, with a scowl at his brother. "If you ask me, you'll be the talk of the base."

"I'll be anyway," Teegan noted. "So at least let's ensure the talk is fruitful."

With his hands on his hips, Mountain stared at his brother, obviously worried about letting him out in the general population.

At that, Sandrine stepped up. "Look. Teegan's getting quite antsy to get out there, and the longer this is kept secret, the more people will know anyway and wonder why it's a secret. Once it's finally announced, and Teegan can get out there and can be seen, the sooner people will calm down," she suggested. "I know we can't defy the colonel, but, in my opinion, the shock of seeing Teegan in the dining room for a meal with everyone would be a better litmus test than waiting on some announcement. Anyway, I get that nobody'll listen to me, but it would be awfully nice if somebody would listen to Teegan."

Mountain snorted. "It's nice that you've become a

champion on his behalf. I'm still not sure I quite understand how you did or did not almost become my sister-in-law," he added, taking a skeptical tone, "but, as a general rule, my brother doesn't need a champion."

"I'm sure your brother doesn't get kidnapped, held captive, and badly injured as a general rule either," Sandrine pointed out, which earned her a glare. "And, champion or not, I sure as hell don't want him attacked again. So, the sooner we sort this out, the better."

Teegan reached over and gripped his brother's hand. "Honestly, it would probably put an end to all the rumors, and, once it's out in the open, you never know. With some of your people dotted around the dining room, watching for reactions, listening, you might see, hear, all kinds of conversations."

Mountain made a sudden decision and then nodded. "Fine, but you're going with me."

"Good." Teegan threw off the blanket and sat up. Instantly he started shivering even though he was wearing a full set of thermal underwear. "I'll need clothes though."

"I'll get them for you," Sydney said and walked to a small cabinet off to the side. "I had Mountain retrieve these from your belongings earlier." She returned with his clothing.

Mountain narrowed his gaze. "If you can't make that walk," he declared a bit too sternly, "or if you decide you aren't up to it, you're staying here."

Teegan glared at him. "I'm fine." With Sydney's help he pulled on the clothes over top of his thermals.

"You're not fine," Sydney disagreed. "However, you are stubborn, just as stubborn as your brother, so I have no doubt that you'll make the trip. However, as soon as you've had your little show in the dining room, you get your ass back here. Do you hear me?"

Her tone was inflexible, and both men knew that she meant it. She returned with his shoes, bending down to get them on him.

Teegan grinned. "I'll take any little bit of freedom I can get," he stated cheerfully. And, with that, he slid off the bed and reached for his brother's hand. As always, it was waiting. He looked up at Mountain and shared, "Don't know if I've told you lately, bro, but I'm damn glad you are part of the family."

"Yeah, I'm damn glad that you're still around to be family," Mountain replied, his voice thick. "Now, let's cut the bullshit and get down to the dining room. I'm hungry." Then he pulled out his phone and made a call.

That startled a laugh out of Teegan, and he agreed. Hanging onto his brother's arm, they walked slowly and carefully to the dining room.

DAY 3 DINNERTIME

SANDRINE COULDN'T BELIEVE that they would let Teegan make a public appearance on the base, especially without the CO's prior approval, but, hey, she understood the sentiment and Teegan's need to get up and out. Plus, something could be said for stopping the rumors running rampant. She walked behind the men, as they headed toward the food. As she got to the dining room, a step behind them, silence fell.

Mountain's voice boomed across the room, making an announcement for all. "Everyone, in case you guys hadn't heard yet, this is Teegan Rode, … my brother. We finally found him."

A round of startled shock, gasps, and then cheers rang out. Mountain finally lifted a hand to calm down everybody. "He's obviously weak. He's not moving all that well, and he'll be a while recovering. So he's staying in the medical clinic, until he's in better condition. In the meantime, rest assured that, in this case, our supposed dead person was not so dead after all."

"What the hell happened to him?" somebody asked.

Another one called out to Teegan, "Jesus, Teegan, what happened to you?"

He gave them a wry look. "If my memory was better, I could tell you," he replied, taking a careful tone. "Unfortunately a side effect of what happened out there is that, at least for the moment, I don't remember much of anything," he muttered. "But I can tell you one thing. I'm damn hungry."

That evoked a wave of laughter, and, walking closely at Mountain's side, Teegan walked up to the buffet area, and there was Chef Elijah, a huge grin on his face.

"Well, damn," Chef said, "now that is a sight for sore eyes. Teegan Rode. … A bloody damn ghost came in from the cold."

"I'm damn glad to be up and seeing you," Teegan replied. "How're you doing, Chef?"

"Better now, and a damn sight better than you from the looks of it." Chef frowned at him. "What can I get you?"

"Food," Teegan declared, "and lots of it."

Chef snorted at that. "I've never been known to starve anybody yet," he muttered.

"And I don't want you thinking it's a good idea now either," Teegan quipped.

Mountain handed his brother a plate, and, with Chef's assistance, they filled it. Mountain carried it and walked Teegan to a table. He sat him down, where a group of people quickly cleared some space for him. He sank to the seat of his chair.

Sandrine watched, frowning to see just how weak Teegan really was. As Mountain returned to get himself a plate, she whispered, "He's awfully weak."

"He is, but he's my brother, and he'll be fine."

She snorted. "That big he-man stuff doesn't always work, you know?" She glared at him openly now, and, when he slanted a look her way, she rolled her eyes. "Okay, fine," she admitted. "It's worked so far, but that's no guarantee it'll always work. Shit happens, even to the hard-asses."

He burst out laughing at that and nodded. "Absolutely, shit does happen, and to people my size too. One of these days you'll have to tell me how you didn't quite make it into the family."

"First of all, I wasn't referring to your size. As for the other, that's a story Teegan can tell you, if and when he can recall the whole thing."

With a chuckle at her spunk, Mountain nodded. "I must point out that Teegan doesn't remember anything."

"I'm glad for your sake that he remembers you," she noted, "because it's kind of a weird feeling to know that he doesn't remember me."

The smile left his face, and Mountain nodded. "I can imagine that wouldn't be easy, unless of course he's willfully dismissing it."

"That wouldn't be so great either," she stated, with a laugh. "Maybe understandable, at least. Honestly, things were fine between us, and, in the end, we both left on good terms."

He didn't say anything, but his gaze searched her face intently. She shrugged and ignored him, then carried her plate over and sat down beside Teegan.

Teegan gave her a cheeky smile. "See? I made it."

"You did make it," she confirmed, "but I wasn't so sure there for a while."

He laughed. "I might have needed my brother's arm a little more than I would have liked," Teegan admitted, "but, hey, the food's here."

"All that to get food, *huh*?" she asked, with a snort. "Don't go making it sound as if I was starving you now."

"I was beginning to wonder if Chef was a little lacking

on groceries."

"Teegan Rode, you know full well that Sydney was trying to get some nutrition into your system that you could handle, without making you sick on top of everything else," she declared. "As for Chef, he seems to always manage to have plenty of good food on hand, so I highly doubt he'll be short-changing you."

"Maybe not," Teegan admitted, "and hopefully now Sydney will let me eat more, but I have to tell you that it's been a pretty rough couple days."

"You better eat up and head back to the clinic, while you still can," she scolded.

He rolled his eyes but then grinned. "Will you stay and look after me tonight too?"

She groaned. "I could use more sleep than that."

"I know," he replied, "and I feel bad about that."

She laughed. "Why? For being injured and weak? Like hell," she muttered. "Eat up." And, with that, she turned her attention to the food in front of her but kept a close eye on him, as he worked his way through his plate.

When he got two-thirds of the way through, he stared down at the food in dismay. "I'm not sure I can finish it. That's embarrassing."

She laughed at the expression on his face. "I can always warm it up for you later, if you want."

He groaned and slowly put down his fork. "I'll give it a few minutes. I could have easily eaten all this before and then some."

"Yeah, but it's not *before* anymore," she pointed out. "It's now and a very different story. You will need to pace yourself, big guy."

He glared at her. "I will get back there."

"You absolutely will."

The meal was excellent, and the conversation jovial, as everybody stopped by to congratulate him on surviving whatever trauma he'd been through. There were several pointed looks, several point-blank questions on anything and everything, but Teegan deflected them all, not letting anybody know exactly what had happened. Of course that would bring about more rumors, but he didn't have any answers, and that in itself was something else.

As Sandrine sat here, waiting for him to catch up and all, she watched as Magnus and Sydney came in to eat as well. They sat at the same table, Sydney studying Teegan with a wary eye.

He smiled. "I won't collapse on you."

"You better not," she declared. "You'll be spending a lot longer in my clinic if you do."

"I'm wondering if I still … Can I have my old room?" he asked in a lowered voice, looking over at his brother.

"Maybe. We'll see."

"Oh, I needed to ask you something else." Teegan got a bit closer and whispered, "Do you know what happened to my laptop?"

"I have your laptop," Mountain replied, "and a USB key."

Teegan's eyebrows shot up, as he stared at Mountain, but no recognition was revealed on Teegan's face. Mountain sighed, then went back to eating. Teegan's gaze wandered the room, looking at everybody, as if trying to remember them.

Sandrine leaned over and asked, "You don't remember most of them, do you?"

He didn't say anything, but several of the others at the

table looked up to see the answer, and he shook his head.

"No, I don't," Teegan replied, "and that really sucks."

"It sucks even more than you know," Magnus stated, "because you won't know who the hell is after you. Without a way to tell friend from foe, you won't know until the blow hits."

"*Great.*" Teegan stared at him. "Are you trying to make me sleep better tonight? If so, you're not doing a good job of it."

Magnus chuckled. "You won't be sleeping without a guard, especially not now that everybody knows you're here. That's just way too easy."

"Something has to happen in order for us to get answers," Teegan suggested, "so let's set a trap and get answers that way."

Mountain glared at him. "You're not capable of handling something like that right now."

"No, but you are," Teegan noted cheerfully. "You know damn well that we need to make whatever break we can get out of this mess. … Trust me. The last thing I want right now is another survival exercise in the great white north, and I doubt that anybody making a second attempt will give me a chance to survive this next time or to give someone else a chance to come along and rescue me."

At that, Mountain looked distinctly uncomfortable, as he realized his brother was talking about Amelia again.

From Sandrine's point of view, she really hoped that this woman was innocent and was just trying to help Teegan, regardless of what Mountain thought, because the idea that yet another shitty person was out there wasn't what Sandrine wanted to consider.

As they trooped back to the medical clinic, Teegan felt his energy fading much faster than he had expected. By the time he got there, he was moving very slowly and needed his brother's support more than he could have imagined. When he finally collapsed on the hospital bed, Sydney was right there to wipe the sweat off his face. "I'm fine," he muttered.

"You're not fine," the doc argued in a waspish tone. "You're exhausted." She looked as if she could bite nails.

Teegan understood her frustration.

"You had your little show, and I let you, but that's it. You stay here now. No more walks for you until I say so." He glared at her, and she nodded. "Glare all you want," she muttered. "You've scared the crap out of me now, and I am not letting you do anything like this again, not until I know it's safe."

"Ha," Teegan replied. "Somehow I don't think you scare that easy."

"No, but watching a patient go downhill, especially as quickly as you have, tells me how much bravado was at play before. So, you won't fool me a second time." And, with that, she quickly picked up the blood pressure cuff and put it on him.

Mountain looked over at him and nodded. "She won't let you do anything now," he noted, a bit too cheerfully.

Teegan glared at his brother. "You don't have to sound so happy about it."

"If it keeps you safe, I'm totally okay to keep you locked up." Mountain glared at him. "Particularly now that everybody knows you're here."

"Oh, come on. They already knew," Teegan argued,

emphasizing with a wave of his free hand. "That's the thing you have to remember in a place like this. The rumors move very, very quickly."

"I know, and I was hoping to confirm that whoever is behind this found out in a controlled way."

"Did that tell you anything?" he asked.

"No, I didn't see any suspicious reactions from anybody. I checked with a few of the others and got the same response."

"And yet not everybody was there."

Sydney nodded. "No, they weren't." Something odd filled her tone. She checked Teegan's blood pressure, then put down the cuff and quickly disappeared.

Teegan watched as she headed to a cabinet on the far side, then checked inside. "My laptop's missing."

Mountain and Magnus stepped up and asked, "What do you mean?"

"I had it here earlier today," she muttered. "Where is it now? I came back from the meeting and got to work, with everybody coming and going, and I hadn't given it a thought." She turned to look at Sandrine, who shook her head.

"No, I haven't seen it," Sandrine replied. "I thought it was here not all that long ago."

Magnus stated, "I saw it too, before we went for dinner." He looked around the room, as the conclusion was pretty obvious. "Somebody came into the clinic while we were all at dinner and took it."

"They might have taken it because of me," Teegan suggested. "Remember? I was using it earlier." He looked over at the doc. "I wanted to check in on news and things."

Sydney nodded. "And that's fine. I gave it to you after

all." She gave a jerk of her shoulders. "I hope you weren't watching anything in particular."

He frowned at her and asked, "Why? What do you mean?"

"It could very well be that whoever took it is checking to see what we know, what you know."

"I don't know anything," Teegan replied in frustration.

"That's what you've said, but that doesn't mean they will believe that. That answer seems too easy."

Mountain stepped up and nodded. "That's true. It's quite possible that whoever took the laptop took it specifically because you were using it, although who would have even known?"

Teegan shrugged. "Any number of people. I can't say that there would have been anybody specifically, but anybody who knew I was here would generally think that. It's not as if the word about me wasn't already out. When you finally made the announcement, all that really did was make it official. The rumors were there, and, although I stayed behind the curtains, a lot of sick people came and went through the clinic. It wouldn't have been that hard to put two and two together."

Mountain nodded.

Sandrine added, "So, we think Sydney's laptop disappeared because somebody was suspicious of what Teegan or anyone behind the curtain might have been searching for?"

"I think so. Nobody's bothered to steal it before now," Sydney noted, turning to look at Teegan.

"I'd been working on the laptop, but I also—" Suddenly he jerked around and then stifled an agonizing scream, as he bumped his bad side. Teegan looked almost frantic, calling out to the others, "Where's the pad of paper? The one I was writing on?"

Mountain looked at him. "We left it near your bed."

"Yeah, well, guess what? It's not here. Somebody came in while we were at dinner, knowing full well that I had been in here, and they've taken both the laptop and the pad of paper with my notes." He looked at Sydney. "Cameras, anything?"

She shook her head. "No. We tried them several times, but …" She looked back over at Magnus.

"The cold was a constant issue. Or they would disappear or be disabled."

Sydney paced the room. Magnus tried to get her to stop but she held out a hand to him.

Magnus added, "The couple times that we did think that the camera would be of value, the intruders managed to cover their faces anyway. So we'll check the hallway cameras, but I wouldn't hold out much hope." He knew too well that this place represented a safe haven to Sydney, and that had been violated again and again.

Sydney was furious, as she muttered, "God damn it. First the missing drugs, then Joy and all that mess. I lost count of the break-ins. I got kidnapped from this place, not to mention Carl was murdered in my clinic. I swear I have had enough of this shit in my clinic."

"Right," Mountain agreed. "I understand how you must feel, Sydney, but we need to stay on track. Focus for now, please." He turned to look at the others. "So, we go for dinner, and somebody comes in, takes your laptop and takes his notepad." He looked back at Teegan. "Was there anything helpful on it?"

"I wouldn't have thought so. Basically it was just me trying to unscramble my brain," he replied. "Not exactly

Earth-shattering revelations. You guys both saw it."

"No revelations for you, but maybe it was to somebody else, … someone who wanted to find out what you know," Sydney suggested. "And maybe that's all they needed."

"Maybe."

Then all the lights in the clinic went out, and everybody went silent.

Magnus spoke first, "I presume the outage is all over the base. I'll head off to the generator room."

"I'm coming with you," Mountain replied, his voice hard. "As for coincidences in this place, I'm struggling to believe it."

Magnus looked over at Sydney and then to Sandrine. "Stay here, both of you, and lock the door."

"Got it," the doc said, her voice quiet, as she looked back over at Teegan. "You know the drill, right?"

He nodded. "I'll stay here, and we'll see what they find."

Sandrine asked, "Does this happen often?"

"I can't say we've had too many of these lately," Sydney replied, "but we've had enough that most people tend to get kind of blasé about it."

"Blasé is one thing," Mountain noted. "What's really nothing to be blasé about is the fact that we have crucial pieces of Teegan's memory missing from out in the wild. Stay with him, please."

With a nod from the women, the two men quickly disappeared, leaving Sandrine, Sydney, and Teegan to wait in the darkness.

SANDRINE WALKED OVER to Teegan for the umpteenth time, and, as had become the norm, he smiled at her reassuringly, in the dim light of the lantern Sydney had produced.

"I'm fine, you know."

"I'm glad to hear that," Sandrine noted tentatively. "A power outage was an unnerving added tension that I didn't really need," she admitted.

"Exactly, and that's why somebody probably did it on purpose," he replied, his voice trailing a bit. "It's kind of smart on their part. Everybody is already upset and off in a way, and this makes it even more so. Anything that keeps things off balance gives them the upper hand."

She didn't say anything and understood the theory behind all that. It's just seeing it, watching it all play out in front of her, was far more upsetting than the textbook version. "I hope that whoever gets their jollies from it gets over it really quick."

He chuckled. "We'll see." He glanced at the door and asked in a calm voice, "Did you guys lock that door?"

Sydney nodded. "Yep, standard protocol whenever something unusual is happening here. That's the first thing I do."

"In other words, it has happened a couple times already.

Is that what you're saying?"

"I guess you must have been too distracted and missed my earlier ranting."

He smiled because he hadn't missed a thing, but they all needed something to talk about while they waited for the power to be sorted.

"As to your question, yes, it has happened more than I would like," she replied, looking at him. "And frankly, it'll probably happen more."

He winced and nodded. "Yeah, wish they hadn't taken my notes though."

"Do you really not remember what you'd put down?" she asked curiously.

"It's not so much that I don't remember, but I was trying to work my way through a couple names and hadn't really come up with anything," he shared, with a shrug. "So, it's not as if it'll help anybody. Yet it might have helped me … maybe."

"I've got more paper if you want," Sandrine offered. "You can sit here and work on that hazy memory of yours, while we wait for the lights to come back on." And, with that, she got up and grabbed some more paper for him.

"I would feel better if I knew that somebody wouldn't get a hold of it though," he muttered.

"This has been another warning for us," the doc muttered.

As Teegan worked on reconstructing the list that he had started earlier, Sandrine walked back over to Sydney and asked in a low voice, "Do you really think this was deliberate?"

"I have no idea," Sydney admitted. "We have to assume it's foul play since we had a theft here, but it could be entirely coincidental that the power went out at this time." She lowered her voice, keeping an eye on Teegan. "However, I'm not real big on coincidences."

Sandrine winced at that and nodded. "No, I'm not either, but I would have thought we had a little more going for us than this."

"Don't lose faith," Sydney said calmly. "We aren't alone, and that makes a huge difference too."

Sandrine smiled at that. "You're right. I hadn't really considered that. We have two men out there looking." Meanwhile, as Sandrine thought this would go on forever, the lights suddenly came back on again. She breathed a sigh of relief and walked back over to find that Teegan had curled up and had closed his eyes. She realized that, in the dim light of the lantern, he hadn't been able to see that well to write, though he had managed to jot down a few things. She glanced down at his notes and froze. Whether he'd meant it or not, he'd written down a couple names that she knew.

Then his eyelids flew open. She smiled down at him. "Hey, I was checking on you. The lights are back on."

"I noticed." He rubbed his eyes. "I'll make a trip to the bathroom, if that's okay with you," he said, "and then I think I'll call it a night."

"That sounds good." She tapped the notepad. "How did this go?"

He shrugged. "Seems to me I can't really get what it is I need to get," he replied in a disappointed tone, "and that's more frustrating than anything."

"Understood, and yet I wondered where you got a couple of these names from."

He looked down at them and shrugged. "Why?"

"You know any of them?" she asked him.

"I don't know," he admitted. "It seems some of them are familiar, but … I don't know. A couple of them"—he gazed at the notepad—"I think are …" Then he stopped, looked down at the notes again, as a frown crossed his face. "Did I really write that?"

"I don't know," she said, looking at him. "This is the paper you were working on."

"I was drifting in and out. I was trying to figure out if other names were important. I think I need to contact Mason."

"Okay, and I know that the new investigator wants to see you again too."

"Right. So, I'm assuming you know Mason already?"

"Yes, I know of him," she confirmed, "but I've never met him."

"Okay. And about the investigator, … I'm not quite there yet, not with any answers for him, at least I don't think so right now." Teegan shook his head. "Dinner really whacked me out."

"Get some rest," Sandrine suggested, as she put the notepad off to the side. "When you wake up again, you can have another look. Maybe some sleep will help you make more sense of it."

"I hope so," he muttered, with a harsh look. "I don't know why I wrote down … *Samson*. He's the new investigator," he muttered, as Sandrine nodded. "That doesn't make a whole lot of sense."

"It will," she replied. "Maybe it was just your mind saying you had something you needed to talk to him about."

"Maybe." Then Teegan smiled at her. "You'll need to shift out of the way, please," he added, and she looked around, confused. "So I can get up." He looked at her intently.

Startled, she stepped back with a shrug and helped him to his feet. "Do you need me to come down to the washroom with you?"

"No, I should be fine," he replied, with a crooked grin. "I would like to do that much on my own, at least."

"You made it to dinner," she confirmed, "so obviously you're doing better. However, you were not in a good shape afterward. It's just … let's not go so fast that it sets you back." And, with that, she led the way to the door. She walked slowly down the hallway with him and stood outside the bathroom, while he went in. If he wasn't quite so prideful, she would have gone in with him, but she understood the male mindset.

In the meantime, she was struggling with why he'd put the new investigator's name down. She wondered if she should say something to Mason or wait until Teegan mentioned more about it. It wasn't her place, but, if something would bring this to a close, she was totally okay with it. As it was, while she stood here, the new investigator, Samson, walked up and stared at her.

She pointed at the door. "Teegan's in the bathroom."

He nodded and headed inside.

She heard a conversation going on and realized that Samson had probably gone in to check up on him. Teegan came out a moment later, looking distinctly weaker than when he went in.

Samson stepped back out again right behind him. "I'll give you a hand getting him back to his room, even though Teegan refused my help."

She gave Teegan a stern look, and he nodded. With Samson on his other side, she quickly got her patient back to the clinic and back to bed. Turning to Samson, she asked, "Don't suppose you know anything about that power outage, do you?"

"No," he replied curtly. "I was just checking around to see if anybody else did."

"I haven't heard back from anybody yet," Sandrine explained, "so I just wondered."

He nodded, his gaze hooded, yet something about him didn't quite feel right. Yet she had no reason to feel that anything was wrong.

As soon as she had Teegan back in his bed, she thanked Samson and added in a polite tone, "I have to ask you to leave now though, so Teegan can rest up. Then I'll lock up too."

"Where's Sydney?" he asked abruptly.

"When the power returned, she went out, looking for Magnus, figured everybody would be back in again."

At that, Samson frowned, then nodded, turned around, and added, "I'll see if I can find out what's up too. Lock the door behind me." And, with that, he was gone.

She locked up and slowly turned around the small medical clinic. Even now it was already starting to feel a whole lot more like a prison, but she didn't know whether she was safer inside or outside of it.

TEEGAN WOKE SEVERAL hours later. He looked over to see Sandrine, curled up on the chair, lightly dozing. He coughed, and she bolted to her feet. She took a moment to look around in alarm, until she saw him sitting up, and she came over.

He groaned. "You were supposed to go back to your room."

"Maybe," she said, holding back a yawn, "but everybody's still checking to see what happened to the power. So, I decided I would stay here."

"It's probably as safe here as anywhere," he noted.

"I don't know about safe, but I figured that nobody would be checking on you, while they were all running around."

He stared at her, wondering at this woman who felt so familiar, yet he couldn't place her. "It's really frustrating," he began in a light voice, "to feel that I know you ... but *not* know you. It's disorienting, and so much worse than anything I've ever felt."

She chuckled. "This way you get to know me again, I guess. Let's start all over again," she teased, with a cheeky smile.

"Would you want to start knowing me all over again?" he asked curiously.

She frowned at him. "I'm not sure what you mean by that." Her tone was light but almost deflective, as if she didn't want to have this conversation.

He nodded. "I guess I hurt you, didn't I?"

"No," she declared. "That's not the word I would use."

"What word would you use then?" he asked, curious.

"I don't know," she replied, still looking anywhere but at him. "Believe me. Whatever we had going between us, ... I got over it a long time ago."

"Maybe I don't want you to get over it," he stated, his voice firm.

She chuckled. "Considering that you don't even remember me, that won't wash."

"And yet I remember some things," he pointed out. "Others are sitting there on the outskirts of my memory, and I want to dislodge them somehow, to make everything clear, but every attempt is not working. Something is just stuck there."

"You can't force it," she murmured. "You know that."

"I know, but that doesn't stop me from trying," he admitted, with a smile.

She nodded. "I know exactly how that feels too."

"Have you ever, … ever been injured like this?'

"Injured, yes, but like this? … Nope," she replied, "and I don't really want to be either. That is an experience you can have, and I don't want anything to do with it."

"It's an experience I could have done without myself."

"If only you could remember what you found out before you were taken," she muttered. "That would be way more helpful than finding the tattered strands of our relationship."

"Is that all we had?" he asked. "Tattered strands? It feels as if we had something special."

"I don't know how you felt about it," she hedged. "You asked me to marry you, but you were totally drunk at the time. I didn't take it seriously of course, and, when you got up the next day, it was as if nothing had even happened. Obviously it was the right thing to not even mention it because you soon left for Germany, and I didn't see you after that," she explained. "So, I couldn't have meant too much to you."

And yet something in her voice made him think maybe it meant something to her after all. He wondered at who he'd been that he would have done something so lightheartedly. "Was I shy before?" he asked outright.

She looked at him and shrugged. "Maybe. You weren't

as outgoing as a lot of people," she shared, nodding in agreement, "but you had lots of buddies, lots of friends, male friends to laugh and to joke around a lot." She took her time, as if considering her words. "I don't know that I would have said *shy*, but maybe a bit with women."

"And yet you're a woman," he pointed out.

She rolled her eyes. "Thank you for that." She chuckled.

"Was I shy with you?" he asked in a reluctant tone. "I'm trying to figure out why I would have asked when I was drunk. I'm wondering if that's the only way I could get it out."

She shook her head, taken aback and in a bit of shock. "I don't know. I guess I hadn't really considered that."

"No, but maybe you should."

"Why are you so worried about it now?"

"Because it's a crass thing to have done, and I would prefer to think I wasn't that kind of person," he stated. She could only stare at him in surprise, and he shrugged. "Obviously we had something going, and right now I feel as if I blew it."

"I don't know that you blew it, but a proposal when you're drunk with no follow-up afterward? ... That's a bit too much."

"And I'm also wondering ..." He stopped. "Something about our relationship is rattling around in my brain that's hard to explain."

"Maybe you should try," she suggested. "Anything you can remember, ... anything at all, would surely help explain some of that."

He shook his head. "I can't really confirm it, not until I get all these memories back, but I feel as if maybe I wasn't thinking clearly and didn't know how to handle it. As if maybe I wanted more and didn't know how to ask for it." He took a moment and studied her intently. "I presume we didn't talk that much."

She laughed. "We spent a lot of time in bed, if that's what you mean." She gave him a little shrug. "We did talk to a certain extent, but I think we were just young." She waved her hand, feeling strangely reserved. "I don't think we need a postmortem on it. We were just different people."

"But we're not different people now, right?"

She took a deep breath. "Okay, so what is it you're really trying to say?"

"I don't really know, but I like you," he said, then shook his head, as if chastising himself. "So, if we had something before, I'm wondering if it's worth trying to see if we have something again. That's assuming you don't have a partner, of course."

"How do you know that *you* don't have a partner?" she asked, studying him intently. "Think about it. You're the one who's lost his memory, and you could potentially have all kinds of relationships out there, waiting for you."

He frowned at her. "It doesn't feel like it. There's no woman floating in my brain but you."

"It might not feel that way," she stated, "but that doesn't mean it isn't true. And to even think that somebody might be out there waiting for you is enough to stop me from going in that direction because, if that were me"—she shook her head vehemently—"I would be devastated."

"So, I'd have to wait and find out if I have anybody, *huh*? Is that it?" he asked, a note of amusement in his tone of voice.

She flashed a wicked grin. "Or somebody can confirm that you don't have somebody else in your life," she added.

"I'm really not sure what else to say, but I wouldn't want to be the person left behind, only to find out that you hooked up with somebody else, without even knowing they were waiting for you."

"That's a good point," he acknowledged. "I'm sure there isn't anybody though."

"And why is that?"

"Because whatever these emotions are that I feel right now," he explained, "they're directed at you. So, I don't think I could possibly have these feelings for anybody else, not at the same time as what I'm feeling right now."

"And what if that's just gratitude? Or waking up from whatever nightmare you were put through and trying to find another way to live, another reason to live, a better way to live?" she asked, looking at him intently.

He gave her a crooked smile. "I like your other reason better."

"What was that?" she asked, puzzled.

"That I couldn't remember and that I'm trying to fill in the blanks."

"You are, and I don't want to be a blank that somebody else has already filled in," she noted. "If and when you decide you still want to get to know me after all this, it's a possibility. However, in the meantime …" She took a deep breath and added, "Let's get you back to health. The rest we have a lot of time to sort out."

DAY 4 EARLY MORNING

T HE NEXT MORNING Sandrine woke up in her own room, lying in bed for a good five minutes, acclimating to her surroundings. Then she got up, dressed in her additional layers, and stumbled her way over to the medical clinic, still yawning.

When she popped in, Sydney looked up and smiled at her warmly. "Hey. Did you get any sleep?"

"I got a few hours anyway," she muttered, as she checked her watch. "I desperately need a coffee though."

She walked over to where Teegan sat, his notepad still on his chest. "Hey, how about you? How are you doing this morning?"

"I guess I'm all right. I could use a coffee too, but, other than that, I'm good." He looked up to her face. Her expression softened, and she turned to leave. "But you don't need to get it for me," he muttered. "I can get up."

She shrugged. "I'm going, so, if you want a cup, I'm happy to get you one. However, if you want to go on your own, that's fine too, as long as Sydney allows it."

She waited a second, and, when he didn't say anything, she shrugged and walked away. She looked sideways at Sydney, "What about you? Do you want a cup?"

"Sure, if you're going, coffee would be great."

Sandrine nodded and quickly disappeared out the clinic

door toward the dining room. She wasn't sure what Teegan's problem was, if there even was a problem, or if he had had a bad night or was reassessing everything going on in his world. When she got to the dining room, she quickly grabbed three coffees, then checked to see if any cinnamon buns were around.

Chef Elijah saw her searching gaze, and he shook his head. "No treats this morning. That cold or whatever bug is going around hit my baker too."

"Ah, is Chrissy down now?" Sandrine asked in dismay.

"She absolutely is, and you will all suffer now until she's back," Chef stated, with a big smirk.

"You're not kidding, but that's okay. We'll appreciate it all that much more, as soon as she's back on her feet again."

"That's the attitude." Chef chuckled.

She took a coffee back to Sydney and gave her the news. "Apparently Chrissy is sick now too."

Sydney looked up and nodded. "Yes, I saw her earlier this morning. She's not doing so great. But then, she's also still healing, as is Whalen," she added, with smile. "So, the two of them are basically back on bedrest."

Sandrine rolled her eyes at that. "I'm sure they're horribly bothered by that."

Sydney burst out laughing. "I think they're having a nice little honeymoon together, while they're here," she noted. "I have to say that it's good that some happy people are around here."

"Seems as if there's a bit of *The Love Boat* thing happening around here," Sandrine muttered. "I've definitely seen a few couples."

"Yep, there are a few, of which I am one," the doc declared, with a smile. "And it's certainly made this session a whole lot easier to get through."

"I can imagine, but unfortunately, for me, there are not that many options."

At that, Sydney looked at her with amusement and nodded toward Teegan.

Sandrine flushed and shrugged but deliberately kept herself quiet, instead of blurting out what was on her mind, which often got her into trouble. Deciding to change the subject, she added, "Since I've been here, I have only seen the dogs once. I thought maybe I would head over there today."

At that came a startled sound behind her. She turned to see Teegan up on his feet, slowly walking. "If you're going over, I'm going too," he said. "I want to see Kosta."

"Ah, Kosta?" she repeated, with a beaming smile. "He's my favorite." She looked back at Sydney and then to Teegan. "I know we're not supposed to get too attached but ..."

Teegan smiled, a gentleness on his face that she could only wonder at. "He's one of the dogs that I was working with before I disappeared," he shared. "I was even joking to Joe about taking Kosta off his hands. He's talking about retiring after this trip, and that many dogs, who will no longer be working animals, is a lot to care for. I am quite pissed off to hear that not one but two dogs were shot." He flashed a boyish grin. "And yes, more memories are coming back."

Sandrine winced. "Well, the last part is great. The information on the dogs is not. I hope they are okay. Otherwise I really don't want to go over there. I'm not up for seeing hurt animals."

Sydney reassured her. "They are both doing much better, and, as Joe has mentioned, he's been out doing some training with them, helping them to work their muscles and to return to full strength." She looked at Teegan and nodded. "It might be a good idea for you to visit them."

He looked surprised. "Why is that?"

"A completely different environment like that? Who knows. It might bring back something else," she suggested in a cheerful voice. "But don't go alone. And I mean don't go *alone*-alone. You need to have somebody who's got the strength to bring you back." Teegan glared at her, and she nodded. "Otherwise I'm not clearing you," she stated calmly, as his expression turned from annoyed to understanding to dismayed. "So, you decide."

"What about me? Can't I go along?" Sandrine asked.

"You can go," Sydney agreed, "but you're not strong enough to get Teegan back up on his feet, should he go down. Remember. It's damn cold getting over there and back, and it takes just ten minutes for hypothermia to set in."

At that moment, Barret poked his head in. "I heard someone bossing people around and totally expected it to be you, Doc. Anything I can do to help?"

"Yep, that would be me, as you well know. Are you doing anything right now? Teegan wants to go see Kosta. However, I don't want him going alone, not without anybody strong enough to get Teegan back here, especially if you must carry him."

Barret nodded at her, then faced Teegan. "Damn, that's a good idea. Come on. Let's go."

"Yeah, I'm not moving that quickly," Teegan admitted, "and she seems to think I'll collapse in the cold, so thanks for the assist."

Barret turned and looked at Sydney, his eyebrows raised.

She shrugged. "I'm not saying he'll step out and keel over. I'm saying that he may not be strong enough to get there and back, due to the added effects of the cold. I don't want him getting partway and running out of steam. Jerry and Scott were enough cautionary tales for me, and I can't allow Teegan to go out there without backup."

"Got it," Barret confirmed. "I'll bring him back."

At that, Sydney turned and looked at Sandrine. "You may as well go with him," she suggested. "You're going stir-crazy in here anyway."

"Ha, it's not so much stir-crazy," she clarified. "I'm just trying to figure out what to do with all this."

As Teegan and Barret headed for the door, she turned back to Sydney. "What happened to Scott and Jerry?"

"They both died of cold out in the frozen tundra. You better make damn sure you don't follow in their footsteps."

Sandrine didn't plan on it, but that was warning enough for her.

TEEGAN WALKED SLOWLY toward the gear room, Barret at his side. Following close behind them, almost close enough to catch him if he fell, was Sandrine. He looked back at her, and she smiled.

"I'm here," she said.

Teegan nodded and kept on moving. It was slow progress, but he was proud of getting up and moving around. As soon as they got fully dressed for the cold weather, they stepped outside, and he felt the shivers set in. Still, he gritted himself against it and determinedly pushed on, until they made it to Joe's area and the dog barn.

When Teegan stepped inside, Joe took one look at him, bounced to his feet with a yell, and raced over. His hug, though enthusiastic, was gentle.

"Good God, man," Joe greeted him, staring at Teegan in shock. "It's so damn good to see you."

He smiled at the older man. "It's really good to see you, Joe," Teegan replied warmly. "You have no idea how badly I was trying to get back again."

"Jesus, I can't begin to think what could possibly have happened to you that kept you away this long, yet you made it back," he said, fascination apparent in his expression.

"I wish I could tell you, but I've lost almost all memory of everything that happened," Teegan admitted. "So, there is next to nothing to tell at this point."

Then came several barks. Teegan turned to see the dogs on the other side of one of the fences. He smiled. "I came to see Kosta. I came to see all of them really," he added, with a chuckle.

At that, Joe stepped back and nodded. "Come on then. Let's go get you a dose of happy canine love."

"Oh, I could sure use that," Teegan agreed, as he bent over to hug the twisting canine that tried to wrap around his legs, "but I absolutely wanted to see Kosta. I've thought about that dog a lot."

"It's kind of a sad deal because I've had him for years, but his dogsledding days may be behind him," Joe admitted.

"Yeah, I'm really sorry to hear that. If he won't work anymore, what will you do with him?"

"I don't know," Joe replied. "He's family, so, at some point in time, if I can find a better home for him, I would definitely hand him off as an adoption."

"I'll take him," Teegan declared, without hesitation.

At that, Joe stared at him. "I know you love him, and he loves you too, but—"

"No, I really love him," Teegan emphasized, "and thinking of this guy kept me alive that whole time."

"If he could have found you out there, he would have, so you must have been hidden really well," Joe shared.

At that, Teegan frowned, then looked to Barret. "Something is there, nagging at me."

Barret kept a close eye on him and nodded. "Just let the thoughts come and go," he said, patting him on the shoulder. "Don't try to force them."

He nodded, as Kosta damn-near plowed him to the ground. If it weren't for Barret holding him, Teegan would have dropped for sure. Laughing, he gingerly lowered himself, until he was kneeling.

Knowing that a pack of jumping dogs would cause Teegan huge pain and likely break open his sores, Sandrine had quickly whispered her concerns to Joe, so he didn't turn out the other dogs.

Not that it mattered, as Teegan seemed completely happy with the attention he was getting from Kosta. It was so good to get a nonjudgmental welcome, not seeking anything from him. So much that he didn't even want to leave, and the tears gathered in his eyes, the longer he stayed here.

Teegan looked over at Joe. "I'm serious about this, Joe."

"If you're serious, I'll consider it." Joe shrugged. "God knows that the dog would be well taken care of. That much I believe."

"You know that," Teegan vowed.

"What do you do with a dog when you're gone on missions?" Joe asked, looking at him. "Because that's, … that's not exactly an easy life for the dog that's always left behind."

"I will find a solution," he declared. "I don't know how much more of this military life I'll be doing anyway." He sensed the curiosity of those behind him and shrugged. "I've got lots to sort out right now," he added. "And not all of it'll be easy."

"I don't imagine any of it's easy at this point," Joe agreed. "I'm doing plenty of thinking myself, assessing my role in all this … military life. This mess has definitely changed my attitude on these trips away. Maybe my wife is right, and it's time I park it and go enjoy other things."

"All the more reason to let me have Kosta then."

"One thing I have to consider is that Kosta's pretty bonded to Sasha over there," he shared, "and she's still a good sled dog."

"Maybe, but she's also one of your breeders, isn't she?"

Slowly, reluctantly, Joe nodded.

"So, give me the pair of them, and they can stay together."

Joe's eyebrows shot up, and he said, "We'll talk about it later. I need to think about it, but, first off, let's get you back on your feet."

Teegan buried his face in the dog's fur, as Kosta half climbed into his lap, barking and licking his face. After a few minutes of that, Teegan gave Kosta a huge hug and then looked over at Joe. "I'm serious about this."

"I'll keep it in mind, if and when the time comes," Joe said, with a nod. "God knows I would be sad to lose him."

"But you also know you can't keep them all. Particularly, if you won't be doing these training trips."

He winced at that and nodded. "Yeah. … Let's talk later." Joe sighed. He looked over at Barret. "Did you guys figure out what happened to Teegan?"

Barret shook his head. "The jury's still out on that one."

"What the hell? How does that even happen?"

"It's not even so much that it happened but that somebody managed to keep him out and away."

At that, Joe's face shut down a little bit. "I presume you're talking about that woman, right?"

Barret slowly shifted and turned to face him. "Do you know anything about her?"

"I've talked to her a couple times in the past," he said, with a nod. "I've been up here lots, not just on this trip, but it was early on," he added, waving his hand in a careless motion. "She's got quite the hand with dogs, and she is an accomplished cross-country skier. She even trained to be in the Olympics at one time. But science is her love apparently," he said, with a shrug. "Anybody who can do all that she can do is something else."

"Maybe, but we're also a little concerned about her. Teegan seems to think she's in danger."

Joe turned and looked at Teegan.

He shrugged. "That's the thought I woke up with. I think she needs help."

"Interesting," Joe murmured. "In that case, what can we do?" He turned to Barret. "Surely you guys are doing something. Not that Amelia needs any protection, if you ask me."

Barret nodded. "Not everybody thinks that. Mountain has been out hunting for her because, in order to help her, we have to find her, and she's proven to be pretty elusive, when she wants to be."

"That's because the village is probably helping her," Joe suggested, with a nod. "That's the way of it. She has been coming up here the better part of her life."

"Maybe so," Barret replied.

Joe looked from one to the other and then shook his head. "If you think Amelia's involved in this crazy mess right from the beginning, I would risk everything to go against that," he said. "My dogs aren't fools, and they sure as hell understand human nature. They thought she was absolutely perfect."

Barret asked, "When you were out on a ski trip or exercising the dogs or a training session—you met her?"

Joe nodded. "Yep. She had dogs that she got from the village at the time. I'm not so sure she doesn't have family there," he noted.

Barret stiffened, and Teegan looked at him with a slow nod. "She might have mentioned something about family."

"But is her family helping or hurting? That's the question," Barret asked.

"No idea, and that's the trick. What is her role in all this?" Joe asked.

"She wasn't involved in that deal with Emily and Nikolai," Joe declared. "I would swear to that."

"I hear you," Barret muttered, with a nod. "We need to figure out who did what." He groaned. "We've got so many bits and pieces."

"Yeah, but just think. Now we have one who's not dead and not missing," Joe pointed out, with a bright smile, as he reached over and slapped Teegan on the shoulder. "I have to tell you that I'm so damn glad to see you."

"Me too," Teegan agreed. "It was pretty rough, and I wish I could remember. So, what was this attack you're talking about?"

"That would be among our most recent messes. Don't worry about that now. So, you don't remember anything? So you were drugged?"

"Yeah, and I've got plenty of needle tracks to prove it, not to mention the constant cold and being on the move all the damn time. All I remember is being on sleds and in some snow caves. I don't know why they would have kept me alive."

"Maybe they kept you alive to protect you."

"That's what I'm thinking," Teegan said, with a nod. "I think that part was Amelia."

"But the only way she wouldn't have brought you here," Joe suggested, with sudden insight, "is if she didn't trust somebody here."

"Exactly, and, if she didn't trust somebody here, I don't know whom to trust either because obviously she knew something we didn't."

"Right, and that's a completely different story," Joe murmured. He looked over at the dogs, milling around. "I sure as hell hope she's not involved. I liked her."

Teegan agreed. "I did too," he stated in a clipped tone.

A note of something filled his voice that had Sandrine eyeing him sharply.

He stood up slowly. "As much as I want to stay and visit with the dogs, I'm starting to feel a little on the rough side," he admitted.

"You go lie down now. You're alive, so let's keep you that way," Joe muttered. "Enough shit is going on around this place for a lifetime."

"That's what you mean, isn't it?" Barret asked, looking at Joe. "You've had enough because it's been a lifetime of this shit."

"Pretty much." He nodded. "It's kind of sucks the way it's all working out."

"It is and it isn't," Barret replied. "We also wanted to bring over our latest arrival into this world of chaos." Barret sent a smile to Sandrine. "She came in on the last supply run to help Sydney."

"Yeah, we met earlier. It's a good thing you came too, since everybody's sick over there," Joe muttered. "I don't even go in for meals anymore. Elijah leaves me food outside. I tell him that I'm on my way over, and he hands it to me outside, and I bring it right back here. It's perfect eating temperature by the time I get home." Joe chuckled. "I'm not getting sick, like everybody else is over there."

"It's a virus," Sandrine explained, "so, even if you do get sick, it's uncomfortable for a few days, but, other than that, just stay warm."

"I got the dogs here, and believe me. They keep me warm at night. Even if I didn't want to sleep with them, I wouldn't have much choice, since they're all cuddlers. And, in a place like this, with some shit going on, believe me. The dogs catch those undercurrents and know when there's trouble, and they've never left me alone. Not since I got hurt. Hell, I didn't do that to myself, and I know Amelia sure as hell didn't do it, so you better find out what the hell's going on." He looked at Barret, then narrowed his gaze. "You already know, don't you?"

Barret raised one eyebrow, as everybody turned to look at him. "Let's just say, Mountain and I have some suspicions. It's under discussion, but we must find proof and a way to flush out this asshole," he stated calmly. "That's not so easy."

"No, it isn't."

And, with Teegan on his feet, Barret on one side and Sandrine on the other, they slowly made their way back to the main part of the base. As soon as they walked inside,

Teegan admitted, "Dammit, I'm just tired enough …"

"If Barret takes you back to the clinic, I'll go get you a hot coffee or maybe a bowl of soup."

He smiled at her. "That would be great." Then he let Barret slowly help him back to the clinic. As he got closer, Teegan asked Barret, "You really do have an idea, don't you?"

"We have a suspicion, but it's not very clear, and we can't come up with a motive. It's a little too far-fetched to even be plausible though," he admitted, with a deep sigh. "So no way in hell we'll bring it up, not until we have a better idea."

"It had to be implausible though," Teegan suggested, "because all this is too hard to understand, much less believe. So whatever's going on has to be deep."

"I think it's more than deep," Barret noted. "I think it's old." With that, he filled Teegan in on the happenings from the last several days. He told him all about Eric, and how one of their best and brightest had turned to violence and malice, attacking Nikolai and Emily, getting Eric shot and killed in the process. Barret also filled in Teegan on how they found Carl—who had been helping Eric—sneaking in the dog kennel, holding Joe and Emily at gunpoint, and was eventually murdered in the clinic, probably by a third person helping Eric. Barret also told Teegan about the half-brother connection between Nicholai and Eric, and they found their father's jacket in Eric's possessions.

"So, that's why Sydney was so pissed. No wonder. So, do you think we're back to Nicholai's family again, the loss of his father?"

"Maybe," Barret said, "but there hasn't been a whole lot of talk about that. So how did you hear?"

Teegan frowned. "I think I knew." He stared off in the distance. "It's not new info to me, so whatever it is was something that I used to know. Maybe I'm just remembering it. Something about Nicholai's family but I'm not sure I ever knew the details until now."

"That's disconcerting."

"So, Eric is dead, and you're thinking it's all related."

"It is related, but whether it's related to what happened to you is the question. I think what happened to you is literally because you got your nose into somebody else's business."

Teegan would have laughed if he had any energy for it, but he nodded instead. "I felt as if I was getting close to something, but it felt very much like—" Then he stopped and shook his head. "No, it felt very much that it was too ludicrous, that it was too big, that there was no way to prove it, and that I would need something much more substantial."

"Exactly," Barret agreed. "And, if you get those brain cells of yours working again, we could compare notes and see if we've come up with the same ludicrous and very ugly scenario as we have. We need you to remember, the sooner, the better."

"And I don't suppose you want to tell me now who your ludicrous suspect is, do you?"

"No, not yet," Barret stated. "All that would do is muddy the waters, and then we'll get unreliable intel from that fuzzy memory of yours. If we could find Amelia, that would change everything."

"It might, but it might not," Teegan noted. As he got to the clinic door, he stopped dead in his tracks. "Shit."

Barret stepped up behind him, supporting him. "Oh my God, what happened here?"

They stepped inside the clinic. No sign of Sydney. In fact, nobody was here. Yet somebody had trashed the clinic. Slowly moving his way to the nearest hospital bed, Teegan collapsed. "Man, I can't help you very much, but where the hell is Sydney?"

Then she walked in and gasped. Frustrated and annoyed, she asked, "Jesus, what the fuck happened? Not again, damn it."

"We just got here," Barret told her. "We came back from seeing the dogs."

"I was in a meeting." The doc raised her hands. "Who keeps trashing my clinic?"

"I don't think they're trashing your clinic as much as they're hoping or maybe worried my memories are coming back," Teegan suggested, "and they are. It's just damn slow and very disconnected."

She stared around at her clinic and then raced to the drug cabinet. The lock had been jimmied and broken, but it wasn't open. She swore and looked over at Barret. "This has got to stop."

"I know," he muttered, "but we're close. We are really close."

She stared at him in shock. "Seriously?" she asked, hope in her voice. "What did you find? Did Teegan remember something?" she asked Barret.

He nodded. "It's just …"

"It's what?" she asked, narrowing her gaze at Barret.

Teegan supplied a very vague answer. "It's a very far-fetched idea, one that will have massive implications, and, if we're wrong," he added, "all our careers are completely over." She glared at him, and he nodded. "I know our careers are not the bottom line here, but we need proof, before we start making accusations."

She shook her head. "All I'm hearing so far is excuses, and I'm getting damn tired of it," she stated in frustration. "That drug cabinet has been broken into so many times that I don't even keep the drugs there anymore."

Barret slowly turned, then asked her, "Where do you keep them?"

She frowned at him, then headed out of the clinic to her room, with both Barret and Sandrine on the doc's heels. As she got to her room, she sighed with relief. "They didn't find them. They're in here."

"Jesus Christ," Barret declared. "You have even less protection in here."

She glared at him. "Maybe, but if nobody knows where they are"—she waved her hands in a circular motion—"that's a whole different story and a level of protection I rather desperately need right now," she snapped. "Normally Magnus is here with me. At least when I'm not around, I can usually count on him."

"But he's been out hunting for Amelia as well," Sandrine pointed out.

"I know, and for today that's enough, for everybody," Sydney murmured, pushing the hair off her face.

DAY 4 MIDMORNING

SANDRINE WALKED INTO her room, closed the door, then sagged onto her bed with relief. This pressure had been building, this weird sensation of everything about to blow. Every time she looked anywhere, it seemed somebody was staring at her, only to turn away. It appeared that everybody wondered about everybody else, and nobody had answers, but the overall suspicion permeated the very air they breathed.

She flopped backward on her bed, closed her eyes, and threw her arm across her face, trying to block out the world and whatever nastiness was going on around her. There was hope, especially with Teegan's shocking return, but still, there were no answers. Thus everybody felt another attack could happen at any moment. Sandrine had seen the two dogs that had been hurt—one of the two looked like Kosta—and knew from Sydney that Magnus had been injured in the same incident.

Sandrine didn't even want to ask questions, yet a part of her needed to know just how bad things would get here. Otherwise she wouldn't have any way of staying safe— though it seemed to be a ludicrous thing to worry about. She was on this secure military base, yet what happened when the actual danger was within the compound itself? As a newcom- er, she already sensed that everyone had separated into teams based on their country, a step backward from the international integration that was essentially the point of the whole survival training session here.

The separate teams ate together, worked together, and some played cards together. It was clear that nobody else was really welcome. Everyone was viewed with some level of suspicion, particularly her. She didn't think that was fair either. She had thought that coming in as one of the few newcomers would have made it easier for her. After all, how could she be complicit with all the madness going on at this military base if she hadn't even physically been there for any of it? Instead they viewed her with even more suspicion because she seemingly had the ability to come *and go*.

After a few minutes more on her bed, she realized she would probably be better off going to the clinic, where at least she could see Teegan. She wasn't sure how to react to the reality that he had been missing all this time. The fact that he was flirting with her a bit and wondering about getting back to where they were kind of floored her. It's not what she'd expected when she came up here, but then she hadn't had any expectations and certainly didn't think she would run into Teegan again.

Having no notion of what to expect here was probably a whole lot better than this mess she was dealing with now. She got up, gave herself a hard talking to, then headed back to the medical clinic. She was supposed to be bringing coffee, but there wasn't any ready at the moment, so she had taken a few minutes for herself in the privacy of her own room. Now to stop in at the clinic.

Sydney quickly checked Teegan over again and then announced, "You've been assigned to a room. So, as long as you come in for regular checkups, keep your fluids up, and stay warm, I'll release you from the clinic."

With a boyish grin that made Sandrine's heart melt, he hopped off the bed, picked Sydney up, and gave her a big hug, then put her down a few feet away.

She laughed. "You did that because Magnus is watching."

"Nope, I would have done it anyway," he declared, with an impudent grin directed at Magnus, then a big smile for the doc. "You've released me from captivity."

"*Right*," she said, with a long-drawn-out sigh. "You were *so* not a captive."

"But I was," he declared, turning to look at her with a seriousness that had Sydney backing up, but then he grinned at her. "Just not with you."

She groaned and shook her head. "Obviously you're feeling much better, so go. Get out of here."

He headed toward the door, and, as he got there, Magnus called out, "Do you have any idea where you're going?"

"I'm going back to my old room," he stated. Looking back, he asked Magnus, "Has anybody been staying there?"

"I don't know. Why?"

"Because, in the back of my head, I think I left something there."

"We checked. We checked every inch of that room. Found nothing of use in our investigation."

Teegan nodded. "I need to take a look regardless." Then he stopped and asked, "But I guess I can't get in there if it's assigned to somebody else, can I?"

Mountain stated from the doorway, "I checked it out, and nobody else has been assigned, so you can have that room back, if that's what you want." Mountain had obviously been there long enough to overhear the conversation.

Everybody looked to see the huge man blocking Teegan's escape route from the room. "I would," Teegan agreed, "if you got your big butt out of my way."

At that, Mountain crossed his arms over his chest, raised one eyebrow, and replied, "You could always try and make me."

Teegan frowned. "If I was a little further along in my healing journey, I might take you up on that. However, right now, I'm pretty sure you would whup my sorry ass."

"No doubt," Mountain declared, "but it would also give me a good idea of how you are really doing because I'm not buying this 'feeling much better' cockiness that I'm hearing."

Teegan glared at his brother. "I'm fine."

Mountain snorted. "Yeah, I hear the words, but you don't sound like it."

"You're not chasing me back into the clinic."

"I didn't say I was," Mountain stated. "Yet also no way in hell are you walking around free and clear, without somebody keeping an eye on you."

Teegan rolled his eyes, then they landed on Sandrine. "Sandrine can keep an eye on me," he suggested, with a big grin.

"Right," Mountain asked, "and what will you do if you're attacked again and kidnapped?"

"Somebody will be closer this time and will give me a hand, staying free and clear," he replied, looking at his brother. "I don't know if I thanked you, but, damn, I'm glad you came to the rescue."

Mountain sighed, then gave his brother a quick hug. "Of course I came to the rescue," he muttered.

"And wouldn't it be nice if I hadn't needed the rescue, and you're right. Believe me, you're right. I absolutely wanted to solve this, without needing the rescue," he said. "And that's one of the reasons I need to take a look at my old room and see if I might have left anything behind."

"Evidence?" Mountain asked his brother.

"I don't know, but my instincts are pushing me hard in that direction."

"Let's go then." Mountain stepped back to let his brother out of the clinic. "I'm coming too."

"I wouldn't have it any other way, bro." Teegan smiled. "When it comes to brothers, you absolutely top the charts as the best on that one."

"You're still a little too cheeky at the moment," Mountain noted, as they walked down the hallway.

Sandrine was hard-pressed to keep up. She hadn't been told she couldn't go, and no way she would miss this now.

"Yeah, I am. I've been given a release from the medical clinic," Teegan said, with a smile. "It almost makes me feel as if I'm back to normal."

"Except don't ignore Sydney's instructions and start getting cocky out there."

"I won't." Teegan gave a hard glance to his brother. "Believe me. I have a good idea of what I survived, but I also know how I survived, and I'm not up for another rendition of that scenario." He took a deep breath. "I get that you're all thinking Amelia had something to do with this, and, of course, she did to some degree. I don't claim to know exactly what, but she is definitely on our side. Remember that."

"We don't know either way, not until we find her," Mountain stated, his tone flat. "And I've been out on skis all day."

Teegan nodded. "You didn't find her, did you?"

"No, I didn't, and that makes me suspicious."

"We know that somebody from the village is helping her, but I have to tell you. I'm not really in favor of you tracking her down, just to be all angry and accusatory."

"I won't get angry or accusatory," Mountain retorted in a frustrated tone. "However, she has answers that we desperately need."

"Maybe. Yet I believe she's also trying to preserve herself in a battle out there."

"How can there be a battle out there now?" Mountain asked in a curious voice. "Who else is out there? Everybody, no matter who, has led back to this base."

"Yet still a lot of training missions are going on, aren't there? Plus people are out there on their own. They're allowed to take the dogs on personal ski runs. They're allowed to go for a few hours. They're allowed to go to all kinds of places. Hell, even the colonel," Teegan noted, with an eyeroll, "got off his butt and was out there."

Mountain seemed startled. "Was he?"

"Sure, even Chef. He was out with Avalon one day."

Mountain pondered that and then nodded. "I guess everybody is getting out for some fresh air."

"And they're training too. Remember that," Teegan stated, with a frown at his brother. "And that kind of training gives anybody all kinds of options."

"And yet what kind of training are you referring to? What kind of options does it give them, aside from the standard survival skills?" And then he stopped and frowned. "Were you working on a message system with Amelia?"

"I wasn't, no. Yet I did wonder if she had a special message system going on out there."

Mountain slowly nodded. "Why? Did you see something?"

"I did, and I left a message," he shared in a strained tone. "I'm sure that I didn't do it quite the way she would have, so the suspicion is whether she will know it was me or not," he admitted. "She may have been messaging, utilizing somebody at the village. I know I would have."

"We all would have," Mountain agreed, with a nod. "We would have used any ally we had, particularly if Amelia's so adamant about not coming to the base."

"We already know she is avoiding the base," Teegan stated. "And, given everything that's happened, apparently with good reason."

Mountain nodded.

They made it to Teegan's room, and Teegan knocked, in case someone was in there, then pushed open the door. No one was there, and no one appeared to have been here for a while. He gave a happy sigh. "Look at that. My own space again," he said, with a grin.

"You make it sound as if it's been such a hardship to be in the clinic."

"Honestly, sometimes it is a hardship to be with anybody else, particularly when I haven't had two seconds to literally be me and just be alone," he explained in a cheerful tone, obviously happy to have his space back. "So, it's not that I'm saying anything against anyone. I just want to enjoy that feeling of having my own personal and private space again. It's not something you get a lot of when you're in the military anyway."

Mountain didn't say anything and just watched his brother, as he walked around the room, a big grin on his face.

Teegan smiled and looked over at him and at Sandrine. "It wouldn't be so bad to keep an eye on me in here, would it?" he asked Sandrine in a coaxing voice.

Realizing it was the first time he'd spoken to her, since she'd come to the room with them, she flushed and glared at him. "I don't think you've been cleared for any extracurricular activities," she replied.

"Oh, I'm pretty sure I could coax approval for that out of our doc," he teased, still with that smile. "It's not as if she isn't heavily involved in that particular activity herself."

"Oh, stop, and it doesn't matter if she is or not," Sandrine snapped, glaring at him. "Despite all your lighthearted tone, I don't think you would get very far down that pathway."

He turned and asked, "Shall we try it?'

Mountain snorted. "Sounds as if you haven't changed a bit." He turned and looked at Sandrine. "You can tell him to buzz off,"

She smiled. "He's testing the waters. He doesn't know what he's talking about and hoping that something will come to light."

"Hey, that's not fair," Teegan said, then groaned.

"Why now?" she asked, looking at him. "You and I both know it's true. If I were to take you up on that offer, you'd be running right back out into the cold."

"Maybe not," he said, with a chuckle. "I feel as if I've been there, done that, and really don't want to go back."

She nodded and smiled. "Good point. Now, what was all that about finding something in this room?"

"That's what I was hoping to remember," he said, looking around the room, a frown on his face. He turned and addressed Mountain. "You didn't find any hidden evidence when you were here?'

"I found a USB, with nothing useful to this investigation. So, no, I didn't find evidence, but I'm totally open to the idea that you may have left something. I looked and looked but found nothing here."

"I always leave something behind," Teegan stated, with a nod.

"I know it, and that's why I looked. As far as ciphers go, you were always at the top of the class, but I didn't find anything. And that really worried me."

Even for Sandrine, there was no doubting the emotions in Mountain's tone. The two brothers were very close, even though this mood of Teegan's was odd for her. It was very lighthearted, but it was also almost artificial, as if maybe Teegan was hiding something. She didn't know what though, and that kind of unnerved her. She studied him closely, as he went through the motions of walking through the tiny-ass room, checking under the two beds and looking in all the corners. The room was so damn small that it was almost comical. "So, what is it you think you could have hidden or left here?" she asked curiously.

He shot her a look and shrugged. "I don't really have an answer for that. Just a sense that something was here. If I could have, I would have hidden it here."

Mountain added, "I already found your computer USB key, but it didn't have anything particularly useful." Mountain studied him. "And that surprised me because normally you would have had something helpful on it."

"So, the fact that I didn't means what?" he asked, turning to look at his brother.

"That you thought you could be watched or that the key could end up in the hands of the people you would *not* want it to."

"Right, so ..."

"Right … so, what would you do?" Mountain asked him.

Teegan turned, stared at the wall, the beds, visually checking everything. It wasn't long before his face lit up, and he reached for the metal bed frame.

When he lifted the mattress, Mountain said, "I checked there."

"You did, but I wonder if you were checking for something in particular."

"I was checking for anything," Mountain stated bluntly.

At that, he watched as Teegan took apart one of the old metal posts and struck it on the side. Mountain realized it was hollow inside, and both he and Sandrine rushed to him.

"Dammit," Mountain said, "these are the old ones."

"They are," Teegan confirmed, as he quickly unscrewed one, but it was empty. Mountain helped him, and they unscrewed and checked all four, and, of course, they found nothing, … until they got to the last one.

While she sat here, biting her bottom lip, watching them both intently, another USB key fell out.

Teegan grinned, as he looked over at his brother. "I'm not so stupid after all, am I?" he asked.

And in that moment, she heard the fear. Fear that he would not get his memories back. Fear that he wouldn't get such a big part of his world back again. That's what all the joking had been about. That's what the lighthearted laughter was for. It was all fake, all a front, in an effort to get through this stage of Teegan's worry, the pain, and the panic that he didn't want anybody to know about.

She sighed, walked over, and gave him a big hug, then kissed him and whispered, "You'll be fine, you know?" He stared at her intently, and she nodded. "You will. It will all come back. I believe that."

His shoulders sagged, as he wrapped an arm around her and held her close, his face buried in her hair, and she hugged him right back.

MOUNTAIN STARED AT his brother in shock and delight. The fact that Teegan had found the second USB key was massive. "Let's hope this has what we need," Mountain muttered, patting him on the shoulder. "Come on. Let's go down to my room."

Teegan looked over at Sandrine, and she smiled. "You can tell me about it afterward. I know I'm not really part of all this."

"If you want to come, you can come," Teegan stated generously. "I don't have any secrets from you." She sensed Mountain listening in, and she nodded. "I know that, but I also work here. So let me confirm that Sydney's okay. We've had quite the rush of sick people. And the damn break-in."

Teegan nodded. "Okay, I'll fill you in after a bit." And, with that, he walked down the hallway with his brother.

"INTERESTING FRIENDSHIP," MOUNTAIN noted to Teegan. "I remembered hearing something about her a long time ago, but you weren't involved in any serious relationships recently so it was a surprise to see her here."

"Yeah, apparently I was sweet on her a while back," Teegan stated. "I did ask her to marry me too, but I was blind drunk, and she wouldn't answer me at the time. And then, when I didn't bring it up afterward, I guess she figured I wasn't serious. Maybe I got off too easy at the time," he said. "Now, as I look back on it, I was a fool. But I'm not a fool, and maybe I wasn't a fool even back then. I think maybe I was afraid."

"I don't think you were so much a fool as you probably didn't know what to do the morning after," Mountain suggested. "You always were good at jumping in and then finding a way to hit Reverse real fast."

"I would like to think I've grown up a lot since then," he muttered.

"Enough to go back in that direction?" Mountain asked curiously.

"Maybe. A definite maybe on that one." Teegan grinned. "Nothing like going through what I've just been through to make you realize how much your life has changed and how much you still need it to change some more."

"Oh, I'm with you on that one," Mountain replied. "I came up here to find you, and, having found you, now we need to get to the bottom of this, so everything can return to normal."

"Whatever *normal* means," Teegan muttered. "It seems everything is such a shit show around here, which is another thing I don't quite get."

"No, neither do I."

"And I guess it didn't start that way, but it seems to be unraveling quickly."

"Oh, I wish it was," Mountain said, looking at him. "I wish it really was unraveling. That would give us a much better chance of figuring out what's going on."

Surprised at that, Teegan nodded. "I guess I was think-ing that, if we had more answers, everything would already have come to pass."

"Maybe, but what answers? We don't have enough answers yet to really get anywhere."

"Barret mentioned how you guys had a working assumption. Is that right?"

"We have a concept, but it's pretty far-fetched." He held up the newest USB key. "And now I'm really hoping that you can figure this out."

"Maybe, but I'm not sure that I would have gotten as far as you guys. I mean, Amelia brought me back, and I haven't had any incidents since then."

"That's true."

Teegan looked over at his brother, who appeared troubled. "And yet that doesn't make you relieved," Teegan noted, with a lighthearted tone.

"Honestly, I'm absolutely delighted that there hasn't been any more trouble for you, though we did have the generator incident and then someone trashed the clinic, not to mention that they stole the clinic laptop and your notes."

"Yes, but it feels very much as if somebody's waiting, and what's with all these break-ins at the clinic? I heard there have been far too many."

"I think this one is literally because of you," Mountain stated. "Somebody's afraid that you had information, and potentially still do."

"And yet will they listen to me saying that I don't?"

"Not now," Mountain claimed, "and maybe not ever. Maybe somebody knew about this key. Maybe that's what's causing us so much headache right now."

"I don't know," Teegan muttered. "It seems pretty far-fetched that anybody is still worrying about that, but, hey, I'm willing to see where it goes."

"It's a good thing," Mountain noted, with amusement, "because you're sure not getting out of this one."

"I'm not trying to get out of anything," Teegan protested. "Yet I definitely don't want to go back to the scenario I came from."

"No, and I don't want you back out there either," Mountain stated in a firm tone, shaking his head.

"And yet here I was thinking I could go out on training sessions and see if Amelia comes to me."

At that, Mountain stopped, as he started to open the door to his private room. Mountain turned to his brother.

Teegan shrugged. "I don't think she has anything against me personally. I know she kept me alive, and maybe I don't know why, but, if you haven't found her, … I'm wondering if I know anything or can do to anything to flush her out."

"You're worried about her, aren't you?" Mountain asked, eyeing him carefully.

"I am. I'm very worried about her. I don't quite know why, except I think—yet, in the back of my mind, I *know*—that she's hurt or something and that she did what she could to save me but that she potentially isn't capable of saving herself. She really needs our help."

"And that may be right, but how good is your stamina?" Mountain asked, as he opened the door to his assigned room. "If I did take you out with me, I don't want to have to pack you back here because you couldn't make the round trip." Teegan stared at his brother, clearly offended, as Mountain shook his head. "Don't give me that shit, or that hurt-puppy look, Teegan. You and I know perfectly well what it's like to drag somebody back through these Arctic conditions. I would need you to be fully functioning, particularly for an extended search, if we're to find Amelia."

Teegan contemplated his brother's words for a good minute, as they entered his brother's room. "How about tomorrow? I'm not sure I need to go all that far though."

"Why is that?"

Teegan shook his head. "I feel that maybe … she told me about a place. I don't know. It's, … it's rattling around in my head," he muttered in frustration. "And I want all that information back again."

"Maybe that's what the drugs were for. Maybe to help you lose that memory permanently."

Startled, he stared at his brother, then asked, "Is there a drug that can do that?"

"Sure," Mountain said, with a nod. "Absolutely there are, many of them. The trouble is, by the time we found you, after Amelia had interceded on your behalf, chances are every drug was already out of your system. I do know that Sydney took samples of your blood, but that was a long time after you *initially* went missing. And those samples were shipped off for analysis, which will take even more time."

"Right. Maybe that's why I was held for so long, so I wouldn't remember anything." Teegan frowned. "And yet it doesn't seem to be working. I mean, I found the computer key."

"Sure, but we don't know what's on it either," Mountain pointed out, as they crossed Mountain's room, and he motioned at his brother. "Close the door."

Teegan shut the door and sat down on his brother's bed, while his brother sat at a small table. Mountain brought up his laptop and quickly plugged in the USB key.

"I went to great lengths to hide that," Teegan noted, "but obviously I thought you would find it." Mountain shot him a look, and Teegan smiled. "Or did you not look?"

"Short of tearing down walls, I looked and looked but didn't find that," Mountain explained. "I did try one of the bedposts, but it didn't come off. I figured it was the newer version of those beds. I should have tried all the other bedposts, but …"

Teegan nodded. "Yeah, I know, but I put it there on purpose, hoping you would find it."

Mountain snorted. "Nice trick, but I could have used less tricks and more answers."

"I'm sure I would have, if I'd thought I could get it to you without getting my ass kicked, or even getting killed outright," Teegan added. "Since that's still a problem now, hopefully you'll forgive me."

Mountain didn't say anything, turning his attention to scrolling through the information on the key. "So far it seems to be a repeat of what was on the other one," he said, disappointment strong in his voice.

At that, Teegan shook his head. "I wouldn't have done that. I don't believe it."

"You might have, if you wanted to secure a copy of the information and thought that you might lose it," Mountain suggested. "Still, it was an extreme hiding spot for a duplicate copy like that."

"Exactly." Teegan shook his head. "May I see?" He stepped up, tugged the laptop slightly off to the side, so that he could handle the mouse, then quickly scrolled through several items.

Then he smiled. "The same in a way but not quite the same thing at all, bro," he declared, as he clicked on one file that had the same name as another one, except for one letter, and then opened up several more files inside, until he was down to the bottom. Flipping the laptop to face Mountain,

Teegan pointed. "This one."

And, with that, they both leaned forward to read the buried file. "So, hang on a minute. This says you saw Chef Elijah helping somebody at the back door to the kitchen?"

"Yeah, that's what it says," Teegan replied, frowning, "but that doesn't make any sense to me."

Mountain stared at him. "Yet why else would you have it here?"

"It obviously made sense at the time, but it doesn't make any sense now. Why would Chef do that?"

"To *help* somebody," Mountain stated. "And Chef would help *any*body, even if we didn't agree with it, as long as he thought they were in trouble. I think some missing foodstuffs from the kitchen was Chef's way of helping Amelia a time or two. I've witnessed him tossing food scraps to several dogs, and not all are Joe's. Chef wouldn't let anyone starve, whether two- or four-legged."

"I certainly agree with that assessment," Teegan confirmed. "That's very much Elijah's way, and he would help anyone and everyone, but …"

"But? But what?" Mountain asked.

"I don't know. Something's nagging at me. Yet I can't get to it." Teegan sighed.

"But helping them at the door? … Did Elijah turn them away afterward? And what about Eric and Nikolai? Would Chef help Eric, especially when Eric's been missing for so long? And help Nikolai, who was good buddies with Eric?"

"I don't know," Teegan replied.

"And yet you have Eric's name here and a note regarding his history, and you clearly mention that he was connected to Nikolai."

"Wow, so obviously I knew that they were half brothers

back then." Teegan scratched his head. "It sounded familiar to me, when Barret told me some of the details unearthed during your investigation. But honestly, I don't really understand what I meant by it, not in the context of these notes."

"What you meant by it and what is coming across are two very separate things." Mountain sat back for a moment, then asked, "Where would your research have come from?"

Teegan shook his head. "I *don't* know," he repeated, looking at his brother in frustration.

Mountain stared off in the distance, deep in thought.

"I guess it's not very helpful, is it?" Teegan asked, with a frown.

"The first USB key that I found—and obviously a copy of it is included here in the second USB—did indicate how all the accidents could have been less of an accident and more of a deliberate attempt to hurt people," Mountain shared. "So there is definitely that aspect to it, and that's helpful. I was hoping this second USB would reveal something more specific."

"Yeah, me too." Teegan stared down at the laptop screen, disappointed.

Mountain smiled. "It's still something," he noted, ruffling his brother's ashen hair.

"I'll work my way through it."

"Do you think other information is hidden here?" Mountain asked him.

"Maybe, let me, ... let me work my way through it." Teegan shrugged. "It's my key, and I know you never did like my filing system."

At that, Mountain snorted. "If there was a system to it, I would have been fine. However, you're definitely not very big on organizing." Then Mountain's phone beeped. He checked the text, and his eyebrows shot up. "Look at that. Mason's found something."

Teegan read the text message. "That's one of the names I wrote down."

"What?"

"It's one of the names I wrote down on a notepad. I thought I knew Mason somehow. I told Sandrine about it, but I guess I forgot to ask anyone about him. You've got Mason in on this?"

"Absolutely I've got Mason in on this." Mountain glared at his brother. "He's the one who allowed you to come up here."

"You can't get mad at him for that," Teegan replied in astonishment.

"No, I'm not mad at him for it, but believe me. When it came time to get help, I knew exactly who to call." He got up and pointed to his laptop. "You stay here and go through that. I'll be back in a few minutes."

"What do you mean?" he asked.

"I'll go talk to Mason."

"What? Why? You don't want me to hear the phone conversation so much that you have to leave?"

Mountain gave him a crooked smile. "Yeah, you could say that." And, with that, he quickly disappeared.

Staring in the wake of the storm that was his brother, Teegan went back to the files in front of him. He had a reason for doing this research. The thought that somebody might have given him drugs so he would forget everything was pretty incomprehensible in his world. Yet the evidence definitely made it look that way, and that made him even leerier about all this. Still, he had to go through the material on this USB, if for no other reason than to digest the information and to try to nudge his memory regarding whatever the hell he'd found, and why he'd even gone looking for it.

DAY 4 NOONISH

THE DAY WENT by very slowly. Sandrine kept looking around to see if Teegan would come back to fill her in on whatever they found in his room. As the day wore on, her anxiety increased.

Finally Sydney looked at her nurse and smiled. "Why don't you go get a coffee and check on Teegan? It's quiet right now, and, honest to God, it's not that you're useless," she noted in a teasing tone, with a smirk on her face, "but you're kind of useless when distracted."

Sandrine flushed. "Oh my God, I'm so sorry, … but, yeah, I can't get him off my mind."

"Go check on him," the doc said. "We've got to listen to our instincts when it comes to things up here."

"Thank you," Sandrine muttered. "Everything feels so wrong all of a sudden."

"I hear you, and that's why I am letting you go. I've been watching you for a while, and you're even making me nervous. Go confirm that everything's good," she suggested, with a half smile. "Just make sure you come back."

With a laugh at that, Sandrine quickly raced to Teegan's room, but he wasn't there. Frowning, she headed to the dining room area, and again he wasn't there either. The new investigator was there, talking to Chef, and neither of them looked to be particularly happy at the moment. So Sandrine grabbed a coffee for herself and one for Sydney and headed back to the clinic. In the back of her mind, she wondered if she should check Moutain's room for them only decided against it as she'd already been gone so long.

When she walked in, she shook her head at Sydney. "He's not there, of course, nor is he in the kitchen," she shared. "I'm not sure where he could be." When Sydney looked at her in concern, Sandrine shrugged. "I know he's probably fine. I just … It's kind of irritating."

"Yeah, it's more than irritating," Sydney noted, with a grimace. "These dratted men, they won't stay where we put them."

At that, Sandrine laughed and nodded. "I guess you could say that. I'm not exactly sure what I'm supposed to do about it, but I guess he'll show up when he's ready."

"Yep, he sure will," Sydney agreed, with a comforting voice. "I wouldn't worry about it. It's not as if he'll go far."

When Sandrine returned to the dining room hours later for dinner, she still saw no sign of Teegan. She stared at Chef Elijah intently and asked, "Have you seen Teegan at all today?"

He shook his head. "I packed them a lunch and understood they were going outside somewhere."

She stared at him in shock. "They? Who are you talking about? Teegan?"

He nodded. "I can see you weren't expecting that."

"No, I sure wasn't," she stated, "but damn. Who is he out there with?"

With this newfound knowledge and spurred on by her fury, Sandrine hurried back to Sydney, only to find her coming for dinner with Magnus. Sandrine stopped them in their tracks, with a furious expression on her face. "Are you aware that they went out?"

"What do you mean, *they went out?*" Sydney asked. "Who?"

"Mountain left with Teegan," Sandrine stated in frustration.

Sydney's eyebrows shot up, and she turned to Magnus, who shrugged.

"It's quite possible," he stated, with a nod. "We're talking about Mountain here, and he isn't bound by the same rules as the rest of us. I had no idea, though he is not required to notify me of his plans. Trust me, I don't exactly approve, but I'm used to it by now."

"Mountain may not have to report to you, but I didn't give Teegan clearance to leave this base," Sydney declared, staring at Magnus, with a narrow-eyed gaze.

"You'll have to take that up with Mountain," Magnus said, holding up his hands in peace. "There had to be a reason, and, if I know anything about Teegan, it's not as if he would have objected."

Sydney winced at that. "That's true. He wants to be in the middle of everything." She looked over at Sandrine for confirmation, who nodded in agreement. Frustrated, Sydney continued, "Yeah, I'll most definitely be taking this up with *both* of them, as soon as they return to the base," Sydney declared, glaring at Magnus.

He held up a hand again. "You can glare at me all you want, but it won't do any good. It's Mountain you need to talk to," he repeated.

Sensing something in his voice, Sydney slowly nodded. "They sure as hell better have had a damn-good reason for pulling this shit."

"I suspect they do. I can't imagine either of them taking

a chance like this, without it."

Sandrine didn't say anything more, and they all slowly made their way to the dining room. She went from ire to fuming to worrying to panic in a matter of a few hours, with nothing she could do about it. Later on, she headed back to Teegan's room and checked again.

When she found no sign of him, she left a note, asking him to let her know when he got back in again, then headed to her room. Less than an hour later, a knock came on her door. She opened it to find Teegan, and he looked haggard.

Relief washed over her, yet she was instantly mad. "Where were you?" she cried out. "Why wouldn't you tell me that you went out somewhere? I've been worried sick."

He quickly stepped inside and pulled her into a hug. "I'm so sorry."

She burrowed deep into his arms, and, although still mad at him, enjoyed the comfort of his arms, her fury tempered by the knowledge that he was safe. Finally, but still furious, she stepped back, looked up at him, and glared. "What the hell was that trip outside for? Where did you guys go?"

Awkwardly he tried to explain. "It was an attempt to see how healthy I was. Plus I had half remembered a location. It was referenced in my notes that we found, but it didn't make a whole lot of sense. So I wanted to go out and see it, and Mountain took me. Of course I knew that, if I ran into trouble, he was big and capable enough to bring me home, if need be," Teegan admitted, his face twisting wryly, acknowledging his brother's size and strength.

"And you couldn't tell anybody beforehand?"

He shook his head. "Mountain didn't want anybody to know where we were—in case we set off somebody here, who might not want us to be out there looking," he explained. "So, it had to be cloak-and-dagger*ish*."

"You didn't let anybody know?"

"Mountain informed a couple people he trusted," he replied in a firm voice. "He had a talk with Mason today too." He studied her, seeing no surprise. "You knew about Mason too then." It wasn't phrased as a question.

She nodded. "A little. People have mentioned him a couple times."

"Why not tell me about him?"

"I had no idea if that was necessary or why you wrote down his name. He could have been a suspect even."

Teegan snorted at that. "Mountain and I talked, and some other information came up with my second USB. Still, Mountain had to check into more stuff. So, we're getting bits and pieces, and it feels as if it's finally starting to come together," Teegan shared, "but I was really worried and wanted to sort this out in my head."

"Worried?"

He nodded. "Yeah, in my head, I figured I had a location for Amelia, something that I was trying to retrieve from my brain. So, of course, I needed something to shake it all loose. I finally managed to do that. So we headed out there to take a look. She wasn't there," he added, "but we left a message, in case she came back."

Astonished, she stared at him. "You found one of the places where you were kept?"

He nodded. "I'm not sure it was where Amelia kept me or where she took me from, but we figured there had been recent activity in the area, so Mountain wanted me to leave a message, just in case."

"What if you left the message and the wrong person gets

it?" she asked, instantly worrying.

He smiled at her. "That's always a possibility, but we left it in her native language. I am told that she originally is from this place."

"If you say so." She frowned, scrubbing her eyes. "God, I was so worried. I asked Sydney and Magnus, but nobody seemed to know anything except that you'd gone out. Sydney wasn't happy about that either. She is kind of irate."

Teegan nodded. "Mountain already made me go get checked over by the doc, as soon as we got back. So I got quite a talking to," he admitted, with half a smile. "I had my fill and figured she should deal with Mountain. Hell, she is a spitfire."

"And yet it doesn't seem to bother you."

"No, because I knew that I needed to do what we did. And now, although I still don't have all the answers," he stated, "I do feel very much as if the answers are there. They're coming in dribs and drabs, but it's okay because I'm finally getting somewhere. ... I don't know if you can understand how frustrating it is to know that all this information is probably still there in my mind but out of my reach, so I can't access it. Yet everybody expects me to know something, but I don't really know anything, and what I did know wasn't reliable," he shared, his own frustration breaking free.

She sighed gently. "I do understand." She gave him a clipped nod. "I had amnesia when I was about fourteen, after a head injury, and believe me. That was a very frustrating experience. So I do understand, and I also get that I'm not in this secret world of yours and that nobody'll give me clearance to get answers, so it's fine, as long as you are okay. I may not like it, but I get it," she stated, followed by a long sigh. She smiled up at him. "I wanted to know that you were okay."

He snagged her again into his arms, then picked her up and twirled around with her, even while she was crying out, "Stop. Stop it, Teegan. You'll hurt yourself."

He burst out laughing in raucous joy. "No, I'm not stopping. I haven't felt this good in a very long time."

When he finally set her on her feet, she frowned and studied him closely, but he did look vibrant, strong, and surprisingly healthy. She shook her head. "For somebody who has only just begun to recover and who looked decades older than your age when you first arrived," she said, "you seem to be doing awfully well at the moment." She brushed his ashen hair out of that familiar boyish-looking face, now with laugh lines around his blue eyes.

"I feel great," he declared, with a growing smile. "I know that nobody else expects it, but that's their problem," he stated, with a chuckle. "I've always been one to snap back very quickly, and, obviously in this case, I had a lot to snap back from. It's taken me a little longer than I wanted," he shared, a wry look on his face. "But the good news is, ... I'm feeling a hell of a lot better now."

"Even after today's ski trip?"

"I got tired, and we rested, but my brother and I used to train a lot together. No better coach I could have at my side than him."

She found herself almost jealous of the relationship between the two of them, which was foolish. Smiling, she nodded. "Did you get food?"

"Nope, and I was hoping you would come help me coax some food out of Elijah. He can be grumpy at times."

"So, you need me to soften the blow, *huh*?" She walked

over and opened the door. "Come on then. Let's get going, since most of the food will be put away by now. He won't be all that happy with your little trip outside either." She noted that Teegan was walking at a normal speed. Amazing.

"He might not be very happy," Teegan noted, with a smirk, "but he did know we were leaving."

"Did he now?" she asked, stopping in her tracks and turning to face him.

Teegan nodded and nudged her along the hallway, toward the dining room. "Yeah. He packed us some lunches."

"Right. I did hear something about that." She sighed. "I swear, my brain's gone to mush. All I could think about was that you were back out there again and that your brother was foolish to take you outside so soon."

"Yeah, telling him that won't go that well."

She shrugged and rolled her eyes at him. "I don't think anybody tells your brother much." As they entered the dining room, she headed to the back and stepped into the kitchen. There was Mountain himself, glaring at her. He obviously had heard every word, and she squared her shoulders. "Yeah, that is my opinion," she snapped. "What were you thinking, taking him outside on a trip like that?"

He took a step forward, but she wasn't one to back down. She fisted her hands on her hips and stepped right up to him and stuck her chin out, even though it barely came up to the middle of his chest. And instead of getting angry, he started to laugh, and it rolled through that great big chest of his, as if deep, menacing thunder.

She stared up at him, astonished, only to find Teegan wrapping his arms around her shoulders, tugging her back up against him, and whispering, "You certainly don't need help in figuring out how to handle my brother because that was perfect."

"I wasn't trying to handle anyone." She glared at Mountain. "I'm serious."

Mountain nodded. "Yeah," he acknowledged in a gentler voice. "However, you also have to remember why I came up here. The fact is, I would never do anything to hurt my brother and would only have taken him out there if I was capable of bringing him back. Always remember that."

She nodded. "I'm glad you have that confidence," she snapped, "because I don't, and, after looking after him for days, believe me, I don't want anything else to happen to him."

Still miffed, she turned away and joined Elijah in the dining room area, knowing the men were chuckling behind her, but they were following her. Elijah stood behind the buffet area, with several plates already set out and filled with food, waiting for the men to get them.

He looked at her and grinned. "Well, have a look at you," he teased. "Not too many people can poke the lion in his own den."

She snorted. "The bigger they are, the harder they fall," she snapped. She took one of the plates and handed it off to Teegan. "Now sit your butt down and eat."

"Yes, ma'am," he agreed, with a bright grin, and quickly sat down at a nearby table. Mountain sat across from them, smirking as she nipped at Teegan, and the two of them proceeded to completely inhale their food.

She looked at him suspiciously, when Teegan finally stopped eating. She asked, "Is that enough?"

"It's enough," he replied, again with a smile.

She looked over at Chef, who was still fussing in the kitchen, and asked if any dessert was left.

Chef frowned at her. "You didn't eat your dinner, so I'm not sure you get any dessert. I've got cinnamon buns for the guys though."

They hopped up and grabbed the treat.

When they returned, Teegan asked her, "Why didn't you eat?"

She glared at him. "Why do you think I didn't eat?" she snapped again. "Because some idiot had gone out in the middle of the frozen wilderness, thinking he was some superhero, without a care in the world for everybody else around him."

He winced at that. "How about having some food now?"

"No thanks," she snapped once more. "I need to sleep." Then she groaned. "I'm just damn glad you're back again."

He nodded. "And I'm damn glad you care."

She snorted. "Don't even get me started."

"I won't," he said, with a beatific smile on his face, "but it is a nice thing to see."

She rolled her eyes at that. "Yeah, not so nice from here." She sighed, then looked over at Mountain to find him grinning broadly. "Don't you have somewhere to be?"

"Nope," he declared, as he eyed her, with a knowing smile. "Now I'm kind of sad he didn't go through with adding you to the family." Mountain stood up, patted his brother on the shoulder, and walked out.

Surprised, she looked at Teegan and asked, "Jesus, will I ever hear the end of it?"

"Hey, that was his way of giving the seal of approval to having you join the family. He likes you, and he thinks you've got spunk. And, if there's one thing my brother likes, it's people with spunk."

"*Spunk*," she repeated, rolling the word around in her

head. "That sounds more like a *spitfire*," she stated suspiciously.

"No, absolutely not," Teegan disagreed. "My brother is nothing if not unpredictable, but, where he loves, he loves deeply, and where he's protective? … He'll go to the mat for you time and time again, just as he has done for me," he shared.

"I know. I *do* know that," she claimed. "It's one of the reasons why I trust him because I know he would never do anything to hurt you, at least not *intentionally*," she added, with a sarcastic note.

But instead of being upset, he burst out laughing and smiled. "This has been really good for me," he said, still laughing.

"Why is that?" she muttered, as she sipped the herb tea she'd gotten while the guys were eating.

"Nice to know you care."

"Oh no, we're not going down that pathway," she stated.

"Ah, we don't have to," he said, "because you already did. I don't know exactly where my head was at back then," he admitted, as he took a moment to study her closely, searching for some response. "That drunk marriage proposal probably sank our relationship in the sewer, or maybe I just wasn't ready, but now? … I'm definitely ready to pick up where we left off."

"Oh hell no," she snapped in a hard voice. He stared at her in shock, and she frowned at him. "We weren't in a good place last time." She shook her head. "I'm not going back to a negative place."

Confused, he asked, "Meaning?"

"Meaning that I don't want somebody who'll take off on missions and not communicate with me beforehand," she muttered. "I can't be with someone who will keep to himself and will shut me out. … I can't go through that again. Communication is key for me, so, if you want to get back into a relationship with me, then we must have a few ground rules."

"Such as?" he asked, leaning forward, his eyes alight with humor.

"Talking, and *not* drunk talking. If you want something from me or you've got a problem with me," she said, also leaning forward, "you talk to me about it. You don't go to your brother. You don't go to anybody else. You talk to me."

He nodded. "That makes sense. Next."

She frowned. "What do you mean, *next*?"

"I thought there was a list."

"I'm thinking," she muttered. "However, I feel as if you're laughing at me."

"I'm definitely not laughing at you, sweetheart," he explained, "but it's really nice to know that we're getting all the details out of the way." He squeezed her hands, before picking one up and gently cradling it in his. He smiled at her and added, "And, whatever the terms are, everything you say is acceptable. Even if you have more terms, more rules, and anything else that goes with it, I accept."

She sat back and stared.

"I know that you're skeptical, but I'm serious," he whispered. "It's really nice to know that you care."

"I didn't want to *care*," she pointed out, slowly realizing the truth herself.

"I know," he agreed, "and that's what makes it all the more delicious."

She groaned. "You won't let me forget this, will you?"

"Probably not," he noted cheerfully. "Besides, it's not

often that we find somebody who cares for us, even when we're not at our best."

"You were definitely not at your best back then," she snapped, glaring at him again.

He chuckled. "It's fine. You're fine. We'll be okay. We will get off of this base and have each other."

She nodded slowly. "You say that but …"

"I mean it," he declared, cutting her off, then chuckling. "We're finding out exactly what we need to know right now," he said, "so I don't think the answers will remain hidden much longer."

"And then what?"

"And then we stay here until our assignment here is done," he said. "We'll return to California. We can head back together."

She shook her head. "And then you'll be going off on another mission. What then?"

"Maybe," he replied, "but it'll involve a hell of a lot of training, if I get deployed somewhere. We always have an option of bringing family or asking for you to be transferred to serve with me as well."

She smiled. "So, you really see this as a long-term thing?"

"Absolutely," he declared. "I have no idea what happened last time because honestly, I was drunk, as you say, and I'm ashamed to admit that I have very little recollection of what I did afterward or why I didn't follow through. I'll have to get back to you on that sometime later, I guess."

"I'll tell you one of the reasons why you didn't follow through," she stated, with a wry look in his direction.

"What's that?" he asked, frowning.

"I replied that, if we were getting married, I wanted kids.

And you went seriously quiet."

Surprised, he shook his head. "Of course I want kids," he argued. "At that time though? … Maybe I wasn't ready?" He hesitated. "But honestly, I don't remember any of that."

"You're sure you want kids?" she asked. "Because that's a no-brainer for me."

"Yes, absolutely," he confirmed, looking at her in surprise. "Is that why you thought I didn't show up again?"

She nodded. "That's why I thought you walked. It made me very hesitant to mention having kids in any other relationship, and I don't want any repeat of that trauma ever again."

"And yet, if kids are important to you, then it's important that you bring it up," he noted, with a light tone, "so I'm glad you brought it up."

"I didn't expect to have this conversation again with you," she stated, with a small smile. "And I'm still not sure that this is a good thing."

"We won't know whether it's a good thing or not if we don't go down this pathway," he said, sharing a smile with her. "As far as I'm concerned, it's a very good thing to take this path. I was alone for a long time before coming up here. Maybe inside I knew I'd lost something special."

"Well, I'm glad you remember that much." She shook her head. "You're overly optimistic."

He burst out laughing at that. Chef Elijah came around a few minutes later. "You guys are having way-too-much fun over here," he noted, staring at them. "Anything I should know about?"

"No, not necessarily," she replied, "just reconnecting, after a lot of years apart."

"Ah." Chef smiled. "That is the best kind of reconnecting."

"Maybe," she muttered. "Except what he did today makes me want to smack him one. Hard too."

Chef gave her a big grin. "I won't stop you on that one. Just remember that makeup sex is the best, if you ask me."

She rolled her eyes, as the older man disappeared, leaving them be. As she looked over at Teegan, he nodded.

"I like the idea of that."

"Of course you do," she said, "but I can't say I'm too thrilled about the idea at the moment. I'm still mad at you. Remember?"

He grinned. "Give me five minutes, and I'll change your mind."

"No thanks," she declared, "but, if you're done eating, I suggest we leave his dining room, so Chef can be done too."

"Absolutely." He looked back to the kitchen. He took his plate over to Chef, who quickly washed it. Then he returned and held out a hand to her. "Come on. Let's go."

"I need sleep," she announced in no uncertain terms, a bit tired and shaken. "Now that you're back safe and sound, I'm exhausted."

"I know how you feel," he acknowledged, "but it's all good. Come on. Let's get you to bed."

"Alone," she stated firmly.

"I didn't say any differently," he muttered, with a half-injured look on his face.

She groaned and rolled her eyes. "You didn't need to. You're like a kid in a candy store."

He chuckled. "Except I'm an adult now, not a child any longer."

"That's good to know," she muttered, as she yawned. "So, how's having your own room?"

"Great," he replied, "and, if you want to sleep in my room, that's okay too."

She contemplated the idea but wasn't sure that they would get any sleep, and now the emotional exhaustion had completely wasted her. "I think we would both sleep better alone tonight," she said.

"I don't think I would, but I understand your decision," he told her, as they stopped outside her room. He leaned over, kissed her gently, and whispered, "Get some sleep, and I'll see you in the morning."

With that and a jaunty smile, he quickly walked down the hallway, leaving her alone to her thoughts.

DAY 5 MORNING

THE NEXT MORNING Teegan woke up, feeling a certain amount of peace at having space of his own. He would have been totally okay with Sandrine coming back with him last night, even if just to sleep, but it was also really nice to have some space all on his own, for the first time in quite a few days, since returning to the base.

He shifted and stretched, feeling the familiar pain, but he was doing much better than he had expected. Certainly better than a lot of people would have thought. He had always healed quickly. It was one of the gifts that their family never took for granted because you never knew when that gift would go away. However, as a general rule, his entire family could bounce back from most things, without too much trouble. As he hopped up and quickly got dressed for the day, he headed over to Sandrine's room to find her coming out.

She looked up and smiled at him. "That was good timing."

He nodded. "I was heading for breakfast. You?"

"Me too. It took me a bit to go back to sleep last night. I fell asleep really fast, but then I thought I heard something in the night, and, after that, it was hard to relax again."

He nodded. "Sorry, that couldn't have been too much fun. Why didn't you call me?"

She linked her arm with his and shrugged. "It's all the worries about everything going on."

"I understand that." He smiled at her. "Everybody's a little on edge."

"Are you sure you're safe and nobody's after you anymore?" she asked. "Because that's, … that's what kept going through my mind."

"Now I'm surprised that you didn't come back and check up on me."

She looked up at him and said, "I did."

He stopped in the middle of the hallway and stared. "What? You came to my room?"

She nodded. "Your door wasn't locked, and I checked on you, and you were sleeping."

Dumbfounded, he shared, "I can't imagine any time in my life where somebody could sneak into my room, and I didn't wake up."

"It didn't do me any good to realize that I could do that either," she admitted, "because that just made me more worried about somebody coming after you."

Nonplussed, he stared at her and then slowly turned and headed toward the dining room. His mind racing, he couldn't recall at any point in time when he'd been that careless, and it did bother him. Maybe he wasn't doing as well as he thought and needed the sleep more than he'd realized.

"Was I not supposed to?" she asked, biting her bottom lip.

He shook his head. "Sorry, it's just a little disturbing for me to realize that you could do that without me knowing because I've always been a light sleeper. But the fact that you came and checked on me is really sweet, and, of course, it's okay." He smiled.

She didn't say anything but seemed relieved.

In the dining room, they quickly got some breakfast and sat down. There were several *Good morning* shouts and various greetings from others, which she responded to in kind.

Everybody was friendlier in the mornings, it seemed to Teegan. By the evenings, it seemed as if a heavy pall had settled in on the place, making everybody not as friendly.

This was something he well understood, especially given the atmosphere, but one guy in particular called out and asked, "How are you doing now, Teegan?"

"I'm feeling a hell of a lot better," he shared in good spirits. "I was even outside yesterday for a bit."

"Man, you had a chance for complete bed rest, and you went outside?" he teased. "You must be dying to die."

"I know. I know. I know," he admitted. "I wanted to go check on something though."

At that, several people turned and looked at him. He smiled. "No luck finding anything though."

"What did you expect? If you left your girlfriend out there, I am sure she's pretty frozen by now."

He rolled his eyes at that. "Man, you guys have been up here too long."

"Yeah, you're not kidding," one of them agreed. "You don't have a clue how many times we've asked for a transfer out of here, and we keep getting stonewalled."

"Sorry about that, guys. For me, I'm just damn glad to be back."

"And you still don't have a clue what happened?"

Teegan shook his head. "I know it's hard for anybody to believe, but yeah. ... Some of those drugs I was given were pretty rough. They took a toll."

"You were drugged?" asked one of them in shock.

He nodded. "Yes, and apparently there was a memory-altering component to it."

"Jesus," the guy muttered. "How can you even want to be here anymore?"

"I haven't exactly been cleared for travel out of here," he shared, "and I hear the new investigator is on everybody's case."

"You're not kidding, man. I talked to him yesterday. He's a hard-ass."

"Sorry, I'm not trying to make life even more difficult for you guys."

"Doesn't matter. One more investigator won't make a damn bit of difference. We've had so many already, so many people looking into this shit over and over, that it's just stupid if you ask me."

"Stupid maybe, but maybe not," Teegan noted. "At some point we're bound to get somewhere." Then, almost as if enlightened with a good idea that he knew everybody else would agree with, Teegan added, "As a matter of fact, I think they've made some progress already."

"Seriously?"

Everybody at the table, faces he half recognized, and, even if he didn't, he knew of them. As soon as he turned to face Sandrine, he caught her frown and nodded. "How's your breakfast coming?" he murmured, hoping she'd take the hint.

She nodded too, and she quickly finished her food. It wasn't long before he was walking her to the medical clinic. "That seemed to upset you."

"Damn right. It was suicide," she snapped.

He squeezed her fingers. "I'll take that because I know that you care."

She groaned. "I don't want you setting yourself up as a target."

"And yet, if I *do* set myself up as a target, you and I both know it will be for the best to finally bring this thing to a happy ending."

"*Happy* is an exaggeration. You said you already had something happening."

"We do. Yet we have to do something to trigger a response from the culprit because we don't have any proof, and, as I mentioned, it's still kind of preposterous."

She winced at that. "Fine, but will you please be careful?"

"I will," he vowed.

"Are you going back out today?"

He nodded. "I'll be heading back out with Mountain to see if anybody picked up the message."

"Already?" she asked.

"We're hoping so. It depends on whether anybody is capable of it or not."

"Fine." She shook her head.

As she walked into the clinic, she turned, and he leaned over, gave her a deep kiss, and whispered, "Now hold that thought. I'll be back soon." And, with that, he was gone.

With a happy sigh, she walked into the clinic to see Sydney grinning at her.

"I see that some things are falling into place."

"Maybe," she muttered. "I'm not sure *falling into place* is quite the right term."

"With these guys it never is," she admitted, laughing, "but they're loyal as the day is long, and you could do a whole lot worse."

"I keep reminding myself of that," she muttered. "We had a hell of a thing going on before, but that drunk proposal seemed to bring everything to a halt, and I, ... I had asked a question, also while he was drunk. I didn't get the answer I was looking for, so, when he walked away, I kind of wrote him off," she admitted, with a wistful smile. "Instead he doesn't even remember it."

"Of course not. Back to all those things you need to sort out."

"That's right." She rotated her neck. "They're going back out again."

"I know," Sydney noted. "but, in this case, maybe it's for the best."

Sandrine stared at her in shock, but Sydney wasn't willing to talk any more about it. Their day started almost immediately, with a steady stream of people to be checked on, to get more lozenges, or to see if anything could help them get over this bug faster, as sniffly noses and sore throats were the illness of the day.

By midday, Sandrine asked Sydney, "How come we haven't come down with it?"

"Hey, don't say that," she replied in a joking manner. "It's always possible."

"I know. I know. I was thinking that, with all these people sick, feeling crappy, it's a surprise that we haven't come down with anything."

"I think it has more to do with the fact that we can't afford to be down with it," Sydney suggested, with a smirk, "until you get so exhausted and worn out that your body has absolutely no option but to drop."

That made sense, and Sandrine had often wondered,

being in a medical profession herself, what it would take for some of these things to disappear before the medical providers got sick. She had done pretty well over the years, but, as Sydney had pointed out, Sandrine's body would get worn down, and her immune system would come under attack simultaneously, and that's when things tended to happen.

By afternoon there was still no word from the men. Sandrine headed to the dining room, grabbed a bowl of soup and a thick slab of fresh bread, and scarfed it down way too fast. It felt awkward and uncomfortable to be here in the dining room. Again, it seemed as if those who showed up were either sick or were looking for information, and, every time she looked up, people were staring at her.

She returned to the clinic and muttered, "Your turn."

"That was fast."

"I know. It's just … It seems everybody's looking for answers, and I don't have any. Plus I don't want to get asked. So, a quick in and out," she said, with a shrug.

"Good enough. I'll go down and get something. Maybe I'll bring it back here."

"I should have done that," Sandrine muttered.

"We have inventory to do this afternoon as well."

"Not a problem. What'll that take? An hour?"

"It's hard to say," Sydney replied, with a shake of her head. "I'll head over to my room and bring in the rest of the drugs after lunch."

And that's what they did. By the time they had everything inventoried, and Sydney had replaced everything in the medical cabinets, they were both exhausted and pretty much done for the day.

Sandrine asked the doc, "Is it safe to leave the drugs here, do you think?"

Sydney sighed. "Every time I think it's safe, something happens and proves me wrong. Yet, when I do hide it all away, something else happens and reminds me of the fact that I'm putting myself in more danger."

"Then leave it here," Sandrine suggested. "Much better that the drugs are stolen than you get hurt. No need to get killed over them."

Sydney looked at her, with a quiet smile. "I hear what you're saying, but there's a certain responsibility to having these drugs around," she noted. "So I don't necessarily agree with your take on it."

"Of course not," Sandrine agreed, "and I understand. It's different for you because you bear the responsibility. But still, so many strange things are going on around here that we can't be too sure of what to expect."

"There sure has been."

"Now that Joy and her boyfriend were killed while stealing drugs, do you have any idea who else would be trying to steal the drugs?" Sandrine asked.

"I've wondered about Joe."

Sandrine stopped and stared at her in shock. "What?"

"The ones being snatched lately? ... They're mild painkillers. Those are the only ones that have gone missing recently," she shared. "Joe doesn't come in here very often, so I wouldn't be at all surprised if he didn't want anybody to know that he's still hurting. I wanted to go over and talk to him this afternoon."

"Ouch," Sandrine replied in a hushed tone. "Won't he get in trouble for that?"

"I guess it depends on whether or not I get a clear-cut answer from him about it," she replied firmly. "I don't want to judge him for what he's doing, particularly when I understand he doesn't want anything to do with what's going on over here, but he could have just asked me."

"Yeah, he absolutely could have," Sandrine agreed.

As it was, Sydney bundled up and left soon afterward. When she came back, she had a smile on her face.

"And? What did he say?" Sandrine asked the doc.

She held up the missing packs of painkillers. "He took them, thinking that the place would go to hell in a handbasket. He didn't want anybody to know, and he didn't want to leave the dogs for long. When he came to talk to me, I wasn't here, so he grabbed what he needed, and enough for an overdose at that," she stated, with a wry look. "However, nothing's been opened, and, as it is, … he didn't really need them. He was thinking he'd get some, just in case, but I wasn't there, and he didn't want to hang around and wait," she explained. "So, no, I'm not reporting it," she murmured. "Whether anybody agrees with that or not, I'm not about to ruin Joe's life over one misstep."

"As long as you're good with it," Sandrine said, "that's all that matters."

"I am. He didn't take much, and all he took was low-level stuff," she shared. "I understand his thought process, and he was honest about it, and none of the drugs were opened, so it's fine."

"Good enough." Sandrine trusted Sydney's judgment. "I guess these other scenarios change everybody's behavior, don't they?"

"They really do," she agreed, looking over at her, her tone serious. "Keep that in mind."

Unsure if that was a warning or what, she asked the doc much later, "Did you mean something by that?"

"No, not really," she replied. "Just a reminder that people act differently when they're under stress here, what with all this other drama. Plus, when it comes down to survival, it gets even worse."

Sandrine nodded, not saying anything more about it. When she talked to Teegan a little later, she explained about the missing drugs.

"Oh, I saw those over there," he shared, with a thoughtful expression on his face. "I don't think he was even attempting to hide them. I think he just figured they were there for the taking, and he might need them."

"He got hurt, didn't he?"

"He did. I know that he gets headaches quite a bit and that he doesn't really want anybody to know about it," he suggested. "Maybe that's why he's self-medicating with alcohol. Anyway, I understand what he is going through, at least in a way."

"Just seems there are always these little secrets."

"Absolutely," he declared, giving her a smile. "You know what happens if you report it. You've got reports in triplicate, and everybody's got to document every piece of BS that's happened," he explained, "and that's not something anybody really wants to do. And that stuff is not only on his record, … it's on whoever reports it as well."

"I know," she stated, "but, coming from a medical professional, it surprises me."

"It shouldn't. Yeah, everybody would probably prefer to have everything precisely documented, but the way the shit's been flying up here, if we documented everything, everybody's career would be damaged, and some completely destroyed," he added, with a sorrowful expression. "Absolutely no point because, until you're in these scenarios, you can't possibly understand."

"You think anybody will ever come back here for more of this?" she asked.

"I would hope not. I hope this craziness is a one-off deal. I've certainly never seen anything like it in my career, and neither has Mountain," Teegan shared. "So, who's to say. Something very unique is happening here. They could even be doing some secret research, where we weren't told we were sitting here in a *Ten Little Indians* scenario, which of course would be completely illegal. Still, it would be fascinating to see the results, after the scientists got through checking everybody's brains, because it very much seems that this whole thing might have been a setup from the very beginning."

At that, she froze. They had been sitting together on his bed, and she shifted a bit to look at him, shock on her face.

"Hey, hey, hey, I'm joking."

"But you're not joking," she replied in horror. "You're not joking at all. Is that the far-out theory you're talking about?"

He shook his head. "No, no, no, honest to God. I'm joking," he declared, as he tucked her into his arms and held her close. "I'm sorry," he muttered, as he looked at her face intently, "I forget that you're not used to some of this. Our thought processes. Our humor in dealing with this."

"That's not a thought process, and that's not humorous," she argued.

He kissed her. "Yet it is. We're all just looking for answers, and we have to open our minds and consider even the wildest impossible ideas, especially when we're not getting results. There was a case study done a couple times, where people were sequestered into a small camp for a year to see how they survived in close confines, such as this base. Think about people up in the International Space Station, who go through rigorous training to see how they'll handle small, confined spaces for the long term?"

"Maybe," she acknowledged, "but, if it is an experiment, it feels as if it's gone horribly wrong."

"Or that's part of the experiment," he pointed out, with a note of humor, still trying to play it off. She shuddered, and he squeezed her gently. "Hey, it's okay."

She shook her head. "God, that thought is just too much."

"How did you end up here?"

She shrugged. "Either the wrong place at the wrong time or the right place at the right time," she replied. "Depends on how you think about it."

"Got it," he said, smiling.

"I was just … I had heard a couple bosses talking. I was doing some computer work at the time, and I overheard something about them needing medical personnel, and I volunteered."

"I'm sure glad you did," Teegan shared, a smile on his face. "I'm not sure how I would have come across you again otherwise."

"In theory, if it's meant to be, it would have happened anyway."

"Exactly. That's what I'm saying," he noted. "It's obviously meant to be."

She laughed. "I did volunteer, although I didn't know you were here," she pointed out, "so you better keep your ego in check."

He grinned at her. "Are you sure you didn't know I was here?"

"Positive," she confirmed. "And besides, technically you

weren't here. You were missing and, in the eyes of most, presumed dead." The smile fell away from his face, and he nodded, making her feel even worse. "God, I'm sorry, Teegan. I shouldn't have brought that up."

"No, it's actually a really good reminder that somebody out there cared enough about making sure I couldn't talk or couldn't do whatever it was they were afraid I would do, that they put me through all that torment."

"Yet they didn't kill you."

"I know, and I keep coming back to that."

"If somebody wanted to kill you, … it would have been easy, and, if they didn't want to do it actively, they just had to leave you out there. Instead not only did this person leave you alive but then somebody else rescued you from that situation and also kept you alive. The whole thing is some next-level shit."

"You would think that, if someone goes to the trouble of saving somebody, keeping them alive would go along with it," he stated, looking at her with an eyebrow raised.

"Sure," she agreed, "but Amelia also kept you hidden enough that whoever had taken you didn't know what to do with the whole situation. Didn't know if it was her or didn't know who else might be working against him, and perhaps he was so terrified that he couldn't do anything," she suggested. "It also begs the question of who the hell here would have the kind of freedom to be gone all that time, doing whatever they wanted with you, and not have anybody asking questions."

Reluctantly Teegan admitted, "I know who would come to mind for anybody else."

"Who's that?" she asked, twisting in his arms.

"My brother. He has a special position here, where he's

half part of the base and half not. Also several other people have worked on the team with him who have an awful lot of freedom to come and go as they need to."

Her question stayed in his mind, long after he'd walked her back to her room for the night. When he thought about it, some other people, including Sydney, had access to a lot more freedom than most. Including Chef Elijah. Even the day sergeant had a lot more freedom. As did all the investigators, of which one was dead. Ted was here still, but, despite his presence on the surface, he'd taken Jerry's death hard, becoming a shell of the man he had been before.

Then there was the new investigator, Samson. Teegan had talked to him a couple times. Something was a little familiar about their interactions, as if Teegan had known Samson before—even an odd reaction on Samson's part, as if he'd expected to be recognized by Teegan. That had happened a couple times already, and it made Teegan feel even worse because the holes in his memory made things a lot harder. He lay in bed thinking about it, when a knock came on his door.

He frowned, opened it, and there was Sydney.

"Hey, do you know where Sandrine is?"

His eyebrows shot up. "I walked her back to her room"—he checked his watch—"about twenty minutes ago."

The doc nodded. "I've got a couple sick patients, and I needed her help to hold down the fort, while I go off and check on a few others, but she's not there."

"I'll be out in five minutes." He finished dressing and stepped out of his room to see her standing there, shifting uneasily from foot to foot. "You can't enter anybody's room, not on your own."

She stared at him and then nodded. "I've got Magnus looking for Sandrine right now."

"Then I'm coming with you, although I would rather be looking for her."

"And I would rather you were looking for her too," she confirmed. "For all I know, she's gone to get tea, or maybe she's outside, although God-only-knows why she would be outside, as a hell of a storm is out there." She shivered, wrapping her arms around her chest. Her phone buzzed then. She looked down and read the texts. "Magnus is checking the kitchen and bathrooms, but there's no sign of her."

Fear tearing at Teegan inside, he said, "Let me do a quick check of the kitchen as well. You better stay at the clinic."

And, with the doc firmly locked in the clinic, Teegan raced to the kitchen and did a double-check, but he found only Elijah there. "Hey, have you seen Sandrine?" he asked urgently.

"Nope, and Magnus was here asking the same damn question." Chef's hands were on his hips, glaring at him. "Are you telling me that you let something happen to that girl?"

"I walked her back to her room twenty-five minutes ago. She was supposed to stay in and locked up for the night. I have no idea what the hell—"

"Well, I do," Elijah declared. "Somebody saw you take her back to her room, and that's all it took."

Swearing, Teegan quickly bolted around and added, "Call me if you hear or see anything." He raced toward the medical clinic, first checking on Sandrine's room and then knocking on the doors on either side. Nobody had really gone to bed yet. When they heard that Sandrine was missing, everybody joined in on the search, and pretty quickly they had a full house searching for her door-to-door.

With a roll call done, it was obvious that everybody was here, and even the colonel stood off to the side, glaring at them. Teegan wasn't sure what the hell the colonel was glaring at, except it was another black mark on his record. And then Teegan remembered Joe.

"I'll go out to Joe's. I know she was a little rattled earlier." And, with that, he quickly bundled up and headed out to talk to Joe and the dogs. As he stumbled inside, he looked up to find Joe sitting there, talking to Sandrine. "Jesus Christ," he bellowed.

Sandrine looked at him and asked, "What?"

"The entire place is on lockdown, and a roll call and a full search has been done, and everybody's looking for you."

She blinked. "Oops."

"*Oops?*" he yelled in outrage. He pulled out his phone and quickly phoned Sydney and texted Magnus. "She's out here with Joe." He stepped forward and glared at her. "What the hell were you thinking?"

She winced. "I was trying to get Joe to explain his actions, so that, as a nurse, I could ignore the reality of what he had done."

Teegan stared at her and shook his head.

"I know. I know. It's not even my business. Believe me. I know that," she stated in a clipped tone. "However, it's a medical clinic, and I work there. So I'm trying very hard to understand how this is a thing I can make peace with, since it's so contrary to the norm. I was lying in bed, and it was driving me nuts. So I thought I'd come over and ask him."

"She, ... she has every right," Joe added, looking over at

Teegan. "Of course I didn't realize she came over without telling anybody."

Teegan sagged against the wall, feeling the pit in his stomach slowly closing, as he realized she was okay. "And are you satisfied now?"

"Yeah, actually I am," she said, with a crooked grin. "And, after you've been all panicked about me not being on the base, I guess it goes along with the same nightmare Joe was experiencing too."

"Not to mention the fact that I won't keep my contract here if I can't handle the pain caused by whatever asshole hit me," he shared.

"I'm sorry about that," she said, "but now I'll have to explain to everybody else why I'm here."

Joe looked at her in worry. She shook her head. "I'll tell them I couldn't sleep and came out to see the dogs." She reached down a hand to Kosta. "You really don't need to worry about anything at all, Joe."

Several other people burst in just then, and she groaned when she saw Magnus and Sydney at the head of the search party.

"I'm fine. I'm fine." She held up her hands to calm them all down. "Apparently I did something stupid without realizing it and walked out here without informing anyone."

Magnus stared at her, suspicious. "I think Teegan had the biggest heart attack, but you really worried Sydney too."

She winced, then looked over at Sydney. "I'm sorry."

Sydney shook her head. "It's fine now," she replied in a relieved tone. "I went looking for you because we've got a couple sick people, and I wanted a hand. Now that I know you're okay, I will head off and get back to that." She turned to disappear.

"I'm coming," Sandrine called out.

"No," Sydney replied. "I'll deal with this one alone."

It was obvious that Sydney was not very impressed about something. Sandrine winced and looked over at Magnus. "I really didn't think it would cause this kind of a ruckus. I just came out to see Joe and the dogs."

Magnus shook his head. "Given the craziness of what's been going on around here, you need to let somebody know where you are at all times."

"I'm sorry," she repeated for the umpteenth time, as she bundled up and slowly walked back over to the compound. She looked at Teegan. "I really didn't mean to worry her."

"She was panicked, and she came to my room, thinking you would be with me. That set off the alarms everywhere."

"Jesus, I just—"

"I know," he said. "I know, but it's the state of our world right now."

"She's really upset with me," Sandrine noted sadly. "And that'll make things awkward."

"So, you need to make it *un*awkward. That is important around here at present."

"But more than that, she also knows about what Joe did, and she was okay with it. Whereas I was the one struggling, and that could be seen as questioning her judgment."

"You also have to do what you feel is right," Teegan noted, "but I hope this doesn't cause any more issues."

Sandrine groaned. "God knows that I really couldn't work my way through it, so I just wanted to talk to Joe." She sighed.

"You did, so now you need to tell Sydney that."

"Jesus," she muttered.

"But now, given the stress of what you've put me

through," he shared, "I think you should definitely stay with me tonight." She looked at him blankly, as he nodded. "I'll wake up half a dozen times now, and, if you're not right there, I'll get up and come to your room to check on you."

She groaned. "Fine, but to sleep, that's all."

"Agreed." They headed back to her room where he waited while she got changed, and then he led her to his room, where they curled up in his bed. "Now, let's get some sleep," he whispered, looking at her.

"Who says I'll be able to?" she muttered.

"Oh, I think you'll sleep," he said, with a chuckle.

"I don't know," she whispered and gently curled up against him. "I didn't realize how mad everybody would be. Now I feel terrible."

"And you can start feeling *un*terrible," he said, cupping her face. "You'll need to make peace with Sydney, but, other than that, everybody else will understand. It's a symptom of the problems here, and honestly, a lot of them will chalk it up to your being new here and not realizing just how dangerous going off on your own can be."

"*Great*, so now I look stupid."

"Stupid and alive is better than brilliant and dead," he stated, with a grin.

On that note, she rolled over, curled up against him, and fell asleep.

DAY 6 EARLY MORNING

T**HE NEXT MORNING** she woke up alone in Teegan's bed. It was so strange to be here, and yet it felt right. Moments later, he opened the door and delivered coffee with a hard kiss, only to quickly disappear, saying he was heading out for the day. They'd fallen back into the same habits as before because bringing her coffee in bed was something that he'd always done before going off to work. She smiled, realizing there might be a whole lot in life to complain about, but this wasn't it.

Now she needed to make her peace with Sydney.

Wincing at that, she got up and dressed, then headed to the clinic with her cup of coffee. She hesitated about getting Sydney some, then figured that she'd probably been up and most likely had her coffee fill already.

As she entered the clinic, Sydney looked up and nodded, as she was dealing with a patient. By the time the patient left, Sandrine was sweating it hard.

"I didn't get you coffee, thinking you'd probably had some already."

"I did," she said, her tone curt.

At that, Sandrine took a deep breath. "Look. I'm sorry."

Sydney stopped and looked over at her. "For what?"

Knowing that this was the kind of minefield that would determine their working relationship, Sandrine opted for honesty. "I'm not sorry for wanting to talk to Joe myself," she admitted. "I needed to find a way to work my own head through this. But I am sorry that I didn't tell anyone where I was going. I didn't want to bring any more trouble down on Joe, but I also didn't know how to process your decision to not tell anybody."

Sydney stared at her, and it was hard seeing the doubt in her expression.

"I wasn't going against your judgment," she added quickly, before it got out of hand. "I was trying to understand it. I haven't been here long enough to really see how much of a mess this place is and how untrustworthy we all appear to each other," she explained. "Last night was a bit of a revelation," she acknowledged.

"Ya think?" Sydney quipped, but she relaxed slightly. "So, how do you feel about Joe now?"

"I understand. I also understand that he's almost phobic about coming over here."

She nodded. "I think that's fairly new. I'm not sure where it's coming from, but the longer he stays isolated, the worse he's getting."

"And I think that, from his point of view, he's staying alive by being that way, and nothing'll change his opinion about it now."

"I agree with you there. I personally don't think anything is as black-and-white as all that, but it is a little disconcerting to see how polarized this base has become."

"Polarized, but maybe for good reasons," Sandrine pointed out in a quiet voice. "When you think about it, an awful lot is going on that nobody can really explain. But, yeah, Joe had kept the drugs out in plain sight. And it was just painkillers. I gather he's a little worried about his injury and has been thinking constantly that this will prevent him from completing his contract. I heard rumors he is drinking at night too, maybe self-medicating. Plus, he has bills, and the dogs' expenses also rack up quickly, and, from what I understood from our little conversation, this may be his last trip out."

Sydney smiled and nodded. "When you think about it, almost everybody's concern is the same old thing. ... Everybody has some kind of worry along the lines that this trip is more or less completing a stage of their life. They won't come back to this, or, in Joe's case, he's got the dogs that he has to deal with and has to pay for, and I don't know where that'll leave him. And the isolation he's choosing allows him to dwell on things more than he typically would. He's also drinking, something most people don't know. Drinking alone can depress somebody. Drugs and alcohol don't mix, so I did talk to him."

"Right. Well, again, I am sorry," Sandrine repeated sincerely. "I don't want this to affect our working relationship, but, as a health care professional, I also needed to find a way to make peace with it because it's so contrary to the normal standards and protocols we work under."

"I totally understand that and had some reservations myself, but this is one we need to let go." Sydney looked over at her, smiled, nodded, and added, "I'm okay with what you did, and it shows more honor than a lot of people, and ethics are really important in our work. I hope you can agree with my decision."

"Absolutely," Sandrine stated, with a smile. "The fact of the matter is, Joe didn't even take any of the drugs he stole. He just didn't want to make another trip to the base to deal with you."

"Deal with me or anybody else who might have seen him at the clinic," she noted gently. "Joe is a special soul, and his heart is with the animals. He tolerates the rest of us, only to a certain extent."

"He has a wife though."

"A wife and a couple kids, but it's clear that he's getting even more ornery and increasingly isolated here, as time goes on."

"In other words, he should probably go home to his wife soon."

Sydney nodded. "That would be my take, yes." And, with that, she returned to work.

DAY 6 AFTERNOON

WITH A SENSE of relief, Sandrine settled into the rhythm of the rest of the day, glad to have resolved their disagreement once and for all. As days in the clinic usually went, today was pretty steady. When she looked up several hours later, Joe stood in the doorway, looking sheepish. She got up and walked over to him. "Are you all right?" she asked.

He shook his head, twisting his hat nervously in his hands. "I wanted to apologize," he said, with a sad smile. "You only came over to talk to me because I was an idiot and didn't want to deal with people when I was here before, and I heard you got in trouble over it."

She looked at him and then winced. "Have to love a small place like this, don't you?"

He nodded. "Yeah." He gave her a forced grin. "Hence my not wanting to be over here," he noted, with a short laugh.

"Oh, I get it," she murmured, "but you and I are both doomed to stay here, until it's over."

He gave her a shrug and nodded. "I don't think it'll be too much longer now," he shared. "Technically we were supposed to be done in another week or two anyway, and we can survive anything that long, right?" he asked in a coaxing tone.

She laughed. "No, you're right. We can," she replied reluctantly. "It's just frustrating as hell." He nodded. "Do you need anything, Joe? Are you okay?"

He winced and asked awkwardly, "I could use a few painkillers. I hadn't used any, and then, as soon as all this blew up"—he covered his face in his hands—"I felt that migraine coming back again. Nothing's been the same since the head injury."

She frowned at him, and he saw the look on her face. "I'm fine. If you don't want to give me anything, I understand."

"No, that's, … that's totally okay," she told him. "I can definitely give you a couple things to help with that headache. If it's continuing to bother you, it might be something that needs another look." He rolled his eyes, and she laughed. "Yeah, I know. I can see it. You're one of those guys who never wants to go to the hospital, or to the doctors or anything, right?"

He stared at her, but his grin was wide as he said, "Point me in the direction of any one of these guys here who would."

"That's true," she agreed, with a knowing smile. "This place is full of tough he-man types."

He nodded. "Can't say I fit into that group." He took a step back. "I'm more in the ornery old bastard category." She went off in peals of laughter at that, and he grinned at her. "See? You're feeling better already. So, how did your interrogation go?" he asked her, putting away the pills she had given him.

"I've been trying to keep my head low right now," she admitted. "It's embarrassing, really, and I feel so stupid. A few people have popped in, saying they're glad I'm safe and sound. A couple others have given me hell because I gave them a heart attack, people being people mostly."

"But it comes from caring," he pointed out, "so you'll survive."

"I will, indeed." She gave him a smile, appreciating that he had come in to confirm she was doing okay.

She gave him several spare pills for his headaches and carefully marked it down on the sheet to talk to Sydney about. But Sydney hadn't told Sandrine that she couldn't give them to Joe, so it was probably a good thing for him, considering that he was looking a little on the peaked side. As soon as he was gone, Sydney walked back in.

Sandrine said, "If you'd been here five minutes ago, you would have seen Joe."

She stopped and frowned. "Considering the fact that he almost never comes in, I would say that is a surprise more than anything."

"Yeah, he came over to apologize for getting me into trouble."

Sydney looked at her in shock and then laughed. "Not a bad thing, though I'm not sure he's responsible for your getting into trouble."

"No, he isn't. It's just that whole *not doing so good in the headspace* type thing. He was also dealing with a headache and wanted some painkillers."

"What did you give him?" she asked, all business.

Sandrine quickly pointed out what she had given him and where it was written down.

"That's fine," Sydney said. "I do need to keep an eye on his head though, if he's still having trouble."

"It's not unusual though, is it? If he had a recent head injury, that has to be normal to a degree."

"There are minor head injuries, and those that continue to trouble you," the doc clarified. "Joe passed all his tests with flying colors, so I released him back to his own space and his animals, but that doesn't mean he wasn't faking it." Sydney faced her and stated, "I'm sure you can see how that might be an issue."

"Not only an issue but I can also see him doing that. He's really not terribly impressed with the idea of coming and getting help."

The doc laughed. "No, he sure isn't, but he did come to get some medicine, and he did come to talk to you. I wonder if he timed it so that I wouldn't be here."

"Maybe. I know he was looking around nervously, as if afraid people would blame him for my not being here last night," she suggested, with a shrug. "I'm quite surprised at the number of people who stopped in to either give me hell for what everybody was put through last night," she shared, with a grimace, "or to say that they're happy I'm okay."

Sydney looked over at her, her own smile wry and tired. "You have to expect a certain amount of that, considering that some people were called from their rooms last night to gather in the dining room for roll call, just to confirm you were okay."

"I know. It just ... never occurred to me."

"It will next time," Sydney stated, with that same cheerfulness Sandrine had come to expect.

"Absolutely."

And, with that, the subject was closed.

As Sandrine headed off to get coffee toward the end of the afternoon, she brought back two—for her and Sydney—only to see Elijah in the clinic, talking to Sydney. It looked to be a private conversation, so Sandrine left and waited until he exited the clinic. Then she walked in with the coffee. "That looked serious."

"Not so much serious as just life right now," she replied, with a tired smile.

A little worried, Sandrine asked, "Is there anything I can help with?"

"Nope, not at all." Sydney gave a wave of her hand. "Everybody's got a few issues, but nobody has anything major, and that's good since nobody's leaving until this is settled."

"I'm quite surprised at this point that they even let me in," Sandrine noted.

"It was probably because I was having such a hell of a time," Sydney replied, with a headshake. "If I'd realized everything would have calmed down again, then I might have fought harder to ensure nobody else came on board." She sighed, looking at her. "Work here definitely has the elements of danger pay attached to it," she noted, with a half smile.

"And, of course, none of that was ever even mentioned to me," Sandrine said, with an eyeroll.

"Of course not. If they can get you for free, then guess what? They'll do it without giving it another thought."

Sandrine smiled. "That's all right. It did allow me to find Teegan again after quite a few years," she admitted, "so I'm okay to have him back and to not get extra pay."

Sydney chuckled. "There have been quite a few of those relationships on this base," she pointed out.

"I'm not against it," Sandrine said, with a quiet smile in her direction. "If you think about it, these are trying times, and anything people can find to help them make it through has my vote."

"Agreed. … It's a little early, but it's pretty quiet, so why don't you take off and get a few minutes to yourself."

"You think I won't get that later?"

"Nope, you sure won't. Not once Teegan gets back."

"I couldn't believe they went back out again," Sandrine said, realizing she hadn't been worried sick all day.

"They will go back out over and over, until they find this person," the doc stated, with a forceful gaze. "Far-too-many questions waiting to be asked, … questions that need to be answered. They won't stop until they find something. Both Teegan and Mountain are hard-headed."

"I suppose. And Elijah? I guess you don't want to tell me what he was in for."

"No, it was private," she replied, with a gentle smile. "In this place, keeping everybody's medical issues private is important."

"Even though I'm here as part of the medical clinic?"

"Even though," she added, with a nod. "I do try hard to keep people's issues classified."

Sandrine shrugged, not really caring either way. "As long as he's in good shape to keep cooking and baking, we're fine."

And, with that, knowing that Teegan had Mountain to help him, Sandrine headed to her room and was thankful that she got some much-needed downtime.

TEEGAN STOPPED AND slowly took another deep breath, letting the cold air warm up before it hit his lungs. As his brother stopped and looked over at him, a concerned expression on his face, Teegan smiled. "I'm fine. Better than

I thought."

Mountain nodded, but his gaze was ever watchful.

Teegan and his brother had been out for the third day in a row, checking to see if there had been any movement on the message they left behind. Still, on this third day, there was nothing. Teegan hated that his memories were still foggy and only giving him bits and pieces. Yet the sense of urgency regarding Amelia needing help was ever-present.

As he looked over at Mountain, he said, "It still doesn't make a whole lot of sense."

"Lots of things don't make sense," he replied, "but you and I both know we need to find her and to hear from her, before this goes any further."

"And yet we've narrowed the possible suspects down to a very small group of people."

"We have." Mountain tossed him a look. "And, for that group of people, we need some damn-good reasons for what's happening."

Teegan didn't say anything, but he knew what his brother meant. It was pretty hard to accuse any of these people because they all seemed so ludicrously normal and unlikely suspects in this event. "Mason was also supposed to get us some more information on correlations between these people."

"Everybody knew everybody before this session, except for," he took a moment to add, "several of the foreign team."

"They did switch in and out quite a few times, didn't they?"

"They did. And Nikolai, with his frenemy Eric, has triggered some of this second round of suspicions."

"And yet Eric was here from day one, until he went rogue, and now he's dead. So why is it that we suddenly think he's got something to do with this drama still?"

"I don't know about *suddenly*," Mountain clarified, looking over at his brother, "but, when it comes to sorting out who's involved, it's been suggested that Eric was blackmailing somebody. By the looks of it, … it had to do with Nikolai's father's death. It had to do with somebody who was potentially on the ground over there at the time. Besides, Peter was a father to both of them. That doesn't mean that it's not a case of mistaken identity. It doesn't mean that the blackmail was happening already, and really none of it means anything because we don't have any proof."

"You're really thinking that Amelia will give you any of that?" Teegan asked, with a headshake.

"No, I'm not." Mountain stopped, facing his brother. "Yet I am expecting that she'll know some answers and will add one more piece of the puzzle. Maybe. Or maybe more than one." Then Mountain shook his head. "I sure hope not, but it feels as if we're close, damn close."

Teegan had to admit his brother had always been a very positive person, but this went over and beyond that attitude. "I hope so too. However, it seems to be a lost cause."

"Don't even go there." Mountain glared at him. "I didn't give up on you, and I'm not giving up on Amelia."

Something in his brother's attitude made Teegan wonder. "You've met her before, haven't you?"

"I have. I saw her early on but not for long, and she wasn't close enough that I could read her facial expressions."

Teegan didn't say anything to that for a moment, while he considered the possibilities. "You met her at the village then, didn't you?"

"She was just leaving, and I didn't understand who she was or what her connection was to any of this at the time," he explained. "Of course, if I had a chance to talk to her now, it would be a whole different story."

Teegan laughed. "Maybe that's why she's keeping well away from you."

"Maybe it is," Mountain admitted. "God knows there isn't any other explanation."

"Sure there is, bro. She doesn't trust you."

"She doesn't even know me enough to know whether she can trust me or not," he argued, "and that's more of a problem. If she had trusted us, she wouldn't have kept you out there as long as she did. Besides, she ought to trust Magnus. I don't know how many times he went up to the scientists' camp to keep their generator going. It seems as if Amelia's making decisions without all the information, which doesn't make sense, considering she's a scientist. How long does she think she can keep this up?"

Teegan added, "We don't have anywhere near the information we need either. I don't know even how long she had me, and, for all I know, I was kidnapped back, and she stole me again. We have nothing solid on the timeline for the period I was missing."

Mountain frowned and nodded. "I hadn't considered that, but honestly, it makes no sense. If she took you from him twice, that would mean she would have to know exactly who is behind this."

"So, maybe she's protecting him," Teegan suggested.

"She's a scientist though, not a mercenary. For God's sake, what the hell is going on here?" Mountain muttered.

Without much in the way of answers, they continued to hunt, going through all the places Mountain had registered as having potential. Soon Teegan realized that his brother had absolutely no intention of letting him out of his sight.

As they headed back, turning toward the base, they heard an odd sound in the distance. Mountain stopped and cranked his head to the side, listening intently. Teegan pulled up beside him and asked, "What do you hear?"

"Shots," he replied in a low voice. "I swear to God, I'm hearing gunfire." With that, he took off at a fast pace, heading in the direction of the sounds.

The trouble was, in this cold, sound was often very deceptive. It would come across crisp and clear because of the cold, yet could be quite difficult to track down. Teegan watched his brother, trying to keep up as Mountain raced ahead, almost in a panic, and realized that he likely thought that Amelia was either shooting or getting shot at.

At that thought, Teegan's heart filled with dread, and he raced after his brother, hoping they could find this woman who had saved him. But, after Teegan finally caught up to his brother, he got somber, seeing Mountain looking around in anger and frustration. "Nobody's here."

"There was, though," Mountain bit off.

"Yes, there was, but maybe it was a case of chasing us away from where we were or something."

When shots were fired a second time, Teegan was suddenly flung to the ground, Mountain on top of him, with orders to stay down. When still nothing came a few minutes later, Teegan slowly lifted his head, his brother on the ground beside him. When another shot rang out, hitting not ten feet away, it *poofed* in the snow, as if the shot had been directed specifically into that location, where Teegan glimpsed some plastic white sheeting. A bullet hitting it made a different sound than when hitting the surrounding snow.

Teegan realized that the shooter wasn't trying to kill them at all. The shooter was trying to show them something.

DAY 6 DINNERTIME

SITTING AT A dining room table, eating dinner, Sandrine was partially included in some of the conversations around her. Not completely, but a couple people stopped to talk to her at least. Some others at her table ate pretty quickly and left, but still, she didn't feel quite so isolated, as she had since she first arrived. Maybe because she'd gotten into trouble, maybe because people felt she didn't really understand the dangers.

She didn't know what caused it, but it was a much more enjoyable experience than she'd had up until now. When a shadow crossed her table, she looked up to see Magnus. She frowned at him. "Any word?" she asked in a low voice.

He nodded. "They're on their way back."

She smiled, feeling some of her tension lightening up. "Were they successful, though?" she asked, sensing something in his voice.

He shrugged. "That remains to be seen."

She rolled her eyes at him. "In other words, yes, but I'm not cleared to know, so you can't tell me anything. Got it."

He burst out laughing. "You got all of that from my response, *huh?*"

"Yeah, well, it's been a theme since I got here," she replied. "I get it. I just arrived. I'm a nobody, and, as far as you guys are all concerned, ... I'm not trustworthy. And everybody who has been here is suspicious because I came in, when they weren't allowed to leave."

He smiled. "I guess that makes for a fairly uncomfortable time here, doesn't it?"

"Whatever," she muttered, as she glanced around. "But apparently because I screwed up so badly last night, people are talking to me now. Who knew that's what it took to get people to be friendly?"

Frowning, he sat down beside her. "Have people really been that standoffish?"

She looked over at Magnus and then at the people scattered behind him. "What do you think?"

He winced and nodded. "Funny the things that you don't see because it's not part of your world."

"That's pretty normal for everybody, I would think," she muttered, with a shrug. "Not sure what kind of a statement you were trying to make there, but I'm pretty sure it's just life."

He smiled. "How are you and Teegan doing?"

"If the guy would ever stay put long enough to get better, we might be doing fine," she said, with a smirk. "As far as our relationship, if that's what you're asking, it's fine. Not quite back to where we were, but in a way in a better place. Especially now that he's regaining some of his memories and knows he hasn't forgotten about another relationship, which was my concern." He didn't say anything but continued to work on his plate of food. "Where's Sydney?" she asked suddenly.

He nodded in the direction of the clinic. "She's still in the clinic, said she would be a little while."

That didn't make a whole lot of sense to her, but she nodded slowly. "I gather she had somebody coming in that

I'm not allowed to see."

He smiled. "Did she send you out?"

"Yeah, a while ago. She told me to go off and to have a little time to myself, that, since things had calmed down, it would be a good chance for me to take a little time away," she repeated, trying to shake the thoughts of something brewing at the clinic. "At the time, I didn't think anything of it, but, if you're sitting here, eating dinner without her, that means she's doing something in the clinic that she doesn't want me to see." At that, she rolled her eyes. "I'm telling you, this place is full of secrets."

He stiffened at that. "Any secrets you've heard recently?"

"No, nobody's talking to mem, remember?"

He nodded and didn't say anything, but he continued to eat. He looked around, and several other people came and went, but nobody came over to talk to them.

"I guess you're used to this kind of treatment up here, aren't you?" she asked. "Where nobody talks to you, where they come and go, steal a look in your direction, then pick up speed and scurry on a little faster."

He gave her an odd look and shrugged. "Sometimes that's the way it goes, … particularly with the work I'm doing."

"Right? All that secret investigative stuff, *huh*?"

"Doesn't seem it's very secret if you know about it," he teased, with a half smile.

She shrugged. "But would I know if I wasn't around Sydney a lot?" she asked, with a questioning gaze. "I doubt it, and I'm pretty sure you guys try to keep all that stuff super secret."

He grinned. "And yet super-secret stuff doesn't necessarily stay secret."

"I think that's a fundamental law of a secret," she noted. "The minute you try and keep one, it goes to pot, and everybody knows." She got up, taking her empty coffee cup with her, and grabbed herself a hot cup of coffee and a big cookie. As she sat back down again, Magnus eyed the cookie appreciatively. Sandrine nodded. "They just came out. Sydney would probably want one too, if you're taking dinner back for her."

"I will," he said, as he got up. He smiled at her and added in a smooth voice, "Teegan should be home soon."

"Glad to hear it." She watched, as Magnus loaded up a plate for Sydney and walked out.

Even if Sandrine went to the clinic, she knew she wouldn't be allowed inside. Apparently the identity of the patient was protected, somebody who wasn't allowed to be seen. She wasn't sure who that was, but it could just as easily have been the CO. She was sure that, if he were ill, even with a cold or a flu, he wouldn't want anybody to see him down there. Sandrine waited a little bit longer and then got up, grabbed a cup of tea, and headed to her room, determined to stay there and to enjoy some peace and quiet, while it lasted. Besides, Sydney would call for her, if needed.

Things could get awfully hairy here, changing from one minute to the next. As she walked past the clinic, several people bolted from it and headed toward the main entrance to the base, Sydney and Magnus among them.

Sandrine watched them in alarm. "Do you need me?"

Sydney called back, "No, we're good."

And that was a definite *No, you're not needed* message if Sandrine had ever heard one. Curious, she followed the crowd to see what the commotion was. As she reached the main door, Teegan had just arrived, shedding his outerwear in the gear room. As she got close enough, she noted he was doing okay, but he was exhausted, his face red and tired.

When he caught sight of her, his face lit up immediately.

It was enough to warm her heart and to make her feel as if she were included, and more importantly, meant to be here. She had to admit that, up until now, that was often a state she didn't really recognize. Walking nearer, she asked, "You okay?"

He smiled at her, then nodded. "Yeah, but I am really looking forward to dinner." He looked at the teacup in her hand. "I gather you've already eaten."

She nodded. "I wasn't sure when you were coming back, but, if you're hungry now, I'll come with you and drink my tea."

Sydney, Magnus, and Mountain joined them, and the doc announced, "We'll be eating in the clinic." Sydney hesitated, looked at them, and then added, "If you want, you can join us."

Surprised but pleased, Sandrine nodded. "Fine, I can wait in the clinic, if you two guys want to go get food."

And, with that, Teegan and Mountain took off to grab some food, before it was put away. Sydney and Magnus walked back with Sandrine to the clinic.

Once inside the clinic, with the door shut, Sandrine noted, "I gather they found something."

"Yeah, we're not sure what though," Magnus said, with a nod.

"Teegan's energy levels are pretty low, so I sent him to get food before it was all gone," Sydney shared. "We'll talk to them in a few minutes."

Because Teegan had looked pretty tired, Sandrine's first instincts were to go help him. As she waited a few minutes,

Magnus got up and quickly disappeared. Sandrine looked over at Sydney and frowned.

"Trust them." Sydney spoke quietly. "If there's a problem, they'll let us know."

Sandrine settled back on one of the few chairs in the clinic. "It's just frustrating sometimes."

"It's frustrating all the time, but you do get used to it."

"Do you?" she asked, with a wry look at her boss. "Not so sure about that."

"If you want to keep a relationship, you do," the doc stated, her voice calm. "These guys are heavily involved in something here, and the reality is, we may never be privy to all the details."

"Yeah, it's the *something* part that's a little odd."

"No, it is what it is," she declared, "until this is settled."

"And then what?" Sandrine asked. "Will you stay or ..."

"It depends on what's happening here." She lifted a shoulder. "If the training base is staying open, then I'll be staying because I'll still be under contract for this assignment. However, that doesn't mean that anybody else will be staying, and, in terms of our group, ... that has yet to be determined."

"Ah, right," Sandrine confirmed, finding a smile. "Let's hope that we find a healthy, happy solution to this mess."

At that, the door opened, and Magnus walked in, followed by Teegan and Mountain. He was carrying a tray and so were the two brothers. As they sat down, the beds and tables quickly filled up. Before anybody had a chance to say anything else, the two big men started plowing into their food. She watched Mountain, fascinated as he ate well over half the plate in what seemed to be five bites. When he looked up and caught her gaze, she was still staring at him.

He raised an eyebrow. "Never seen a man eat before?"

"Never seen a plate disappear in five bites before," she replied. "Do you want me to get you more?"

He contemplated that for a moment, then shook his head. "I should be good."

She nodded doubtfully, as he studied the rest of his plate, then looked over at Teegan, who was watching his brother with a grin on his face. "You're both in awfully high spirits," Sandrine noted, "so I gather you found something that's making you happy."

"I don't know about making us happy," Mountain clarified, "but we were shot at today."

At that, everybody stiffened and stared at him in shock.

"But were we?" Teegan asked him out loud. "I'm not so sure that we were shot at, versus somebody was shooting in our direction, trying to show us something."

"What were they trying to show you, if they were shooting in your direction?" Magnus asked.

Mountain looked at him and grinned. "That's the thing. Looks to be another cache in a snow cave. We opened it up and brought everything back with us," he shared, looking around, noting their packs on the far side of the room. "And it's all in there."

Magnus hopped up and brought the bags over where he could slowly unpack them. Almost immediately, he whistled. "Do you recognize any of this stuff?" he asked, turning to look at Teegan.

Teegan nodded. "Yes, a lot of it looks to be from where I was held captive. I just don't know whether it was Amelia's or not."

"So, who is it you think was doing the shooting?" Magnus asked, sitting back. "Are you thinking they were deliberately trying to show you this?"

Mountain nodded. "Yes. They fired all around us and then seemed to really target the one spot. I think they were trying to locate the snow cave from a distance as well, so that we could see it."

"Jesus," Magnus muttered, as he stared at him.

Then came a knock on the door. Everybody froze, and then the knock came again, with a funny staccato. When it opened up again, Barret and Egan stepped in. "Hey," they said together, watching the expressions on everyone's face.

"What happened?" Barret asked in haste.

As they filled them in on the news, Egan joined Magnus to look through the bag. "So, this is the stuff that was being kept there?"

"Yes."

"I'm not sure anything in the bag identifies anyone though," Magnus shared, when he was finally done searching it. "Yet you're right. Anything that gives us one more clue into the location of who was holding you is a big help."

"It's a help. It's just not enough," Teegan said in frustration.

"And, if Amelia pointed this out for us, she appears to be fine," Mountain declared, "still not wanting anything to do with us."

"Not wanting anything to do with you is one thing. Actively shooting at you is a whole different story," Magnus added.

"Not *at* us," Teegan clarified in a firm voice. "Pointing out something to us."

The other men nodded but didn't say anything.

Sandrine didn't think they totally bought Teegan's theory, but they wouldn't argue it either, not while they were still going through things. Currently they were looking at a cup, plate, some paper, a blanket, and empty gum wrappers.

When they were finished, Mountain held up his phone. "Then there are these photos." And he quickly brought them up on his phone and held it out for everybody to slowly go through.

Sandrine was allowed to look as the photos were coming around for them all to see. She studied them carefully and realized it was basically a deserted campsite, with a few items left behind. There was an indentation where maybe a sleeping bag or a bedroll had been and what looked to be the remains of a fire.

"So, are you thinking this is where you were held?" Magnus asked Teegan.

Teegan nodded.

Magnus continued. "What would be the purpose of showing this snow cave to you? If it was where Amelia had kept you, that in itself isn't in any way indicative of who else may have been there."

Teegan replied, "I think it's the one where Amelia found me, and I think she's hoping that, by showing us this specific location, we can sort out who is behind it."

"So you're thinking that she doesn't know the person who took you?" Egan asked.

"Correct," Teegan replied, with a nod. "Potentially she snuck me away before finding out for herself, which would also imply that she doesn't have any idea who my kidnapper was and is, therefore, scared of everybody from this base."

"Maybe, but if she would just talk to us," Mountain began, his voice hard, "we could potentially help her."

"And yet, who does she trust?"

"I don't know. I've left her lots of messages, hoping she

would find a level of trust with me," Mountain noted, "but I can't see that any of that has worked to date."

"I don't agree," Sandrine interjected. "The fact that she made the effort to show you this place and allowed you to bring this stuff back means that it did work. I don't think she would have done it otherwise. She wouldn't have taken the chance of sharing this intel with you if she thought you had been there before."

"Except for the fact that we weren't anywhere near this hidey-hole," Teegan pointed out.

Sandrine nodded and added, "Yet you were out there, looking for something, and, if she's been keeping track of anybody out there in that area in recent weeks, she would have known that you didn't know where this hidden campsite was."

That hit them hard, but she could be right.

ON THE RETURN trip to the base, Teegan had been cold and tired, and the initial thread of excitement had faded. When they hauled the items back to base, Mountain had carried the bulk of it. Teegan carried a little but, adding even five pounds to his load, which normally wouldn't even be noticeable, had suddenly made it all far too much. But he'd gritted his teeth and had kept on pushing.

When he'd come in to the base, his energy was flagging to the extent that Sydney had steered him toward the food and said, "Go." Teegan had stopped, only long enough to speak with Sandrine. When Sydney announced they would be eating in the clinic, Teegan and his brother had headed to the dining room, without even a glance back.

Now sitting in one of the clinic's hospital beds, enjoying a cookie, with a cup of coffee in his hand, Teegan looked over at Sandrine and had a good idea that's where the cookie had come from.

She smiled at him. "They are pretty good cookies, so eat up."

"Oh, he gets a cookie," Mountain complained, looking at her in outrage, "but I don't?"

She reached behind her and pulled out another cookie and handed it to him. He snatched it up, with a big grin.

"See? I told you that she was good people," Teegan reminded his brother.

Mountain laughed. "Yeah, well, you're supposed to do more than get drunk and ask them to marry you. That approach really doesn't work out that well."

Teegan rolled his eyes and saw the flush on her face. "Oh, come on now. You're embarrassing her."

Mountain shrugged. "Doesn't matter if she's embarrassed or not. She'll have to get used to it, one way or another."

Teegan laughed. "It would be nice if we had a chance to *not* scare her away completely, *before* we get her on our side."

"She's already on our side," Mountain declared, eyeing her intently. "She got us cookies. That's as good a ritual as any."

At that, Teegan looked over at Sandrine with a big grin.

"I won't put her on the spot right now," Mountain added, with an eyeroll. "But, boy, you have some making up to do, Teegan."

At that, Teegan looked over at the pile of stuff and launched back into the topic at hand. "Okay, everybody, back on track," he announced, studying the stuff scattered around. "What the hell does all this mean?"

"It means that Amelia's trying to help us," Sandrine stated.

"If she's trying to help us, she's going about it in a very strange way," Barret noted in an exasperated tone.

"As we've already pointed out," Sandrine explained, "that's because she doesn't trust anybody on base, and honestly, can we blame her? I don't even know who can be trusted here. I go into the dining room and basically nobody talks to me, unless it's unavoidable, and then they make a hasty exit. I look around, and I see people, but I don't really know them," she shared. "I see people who are keeping to themselves and almost trying to hide. So, if I'm here on the base, even though I haven't been here very long, I can't even begin to imagine how Amelia feels. She's on the outside, and whether she knows people here, or heard about the trouble here from the people she knows over at the village is a whole different story. Still, the bottom line is that she doesn't know whom to trust, and she's hoping that we'll solve it ourselves."

"It would sure be a whole lot easier if we got some help from her," Mountain grumbled.

"Maybe," Sandrine agreed, "but I suspect that, if she comes in, it'll be because she needs help, not that she's got help to give."

At that, Teegan looked over at her and nodded. "And it's quite possible that whoever is behind all this is hunting her too." He turned, looking at Mountain in frustration. "I wish to God she would talk to us."

"I do too," he agreed, with a frown. "I wish I knew how to convince her to do that because right now she's avoiding us and—"

"But she's taking chances," Teegan interrupted. "If anybody else saw her, saw what she did today, there's a good chance they're on her case now and trying to get her to stop doing whatever they think she's doing. And, if we think she might be helping us, ... there's a pretty good chance that somebody else will make that assumption as well."

Mountain looked at him in frustration. "What do you want me to do, Teegan? She saved your life, supposedly," he said, with a caveat. "Remember? We don't know the whole truth yet, and, for all we know, she's behind the whole thing."

"And yet you don't believe that," Teegan stated. "I know you don't."

Mountain glared at him for a moment. Then his shoulders slumped, and he nodded. "I find it hard to believe, yes, but I also have to question why she's not coming in."

"No, you don't," Magnus argued, holding up a hand. "I think Sandrine's right. I think Amelia's trying to help, yet trying to stay away, because she doesn't want to get caught up in all this other stuff, or she doesn't know whom to trust. And let's face it. So far, we've haven't exactly proved ourselves trustworthy," he admitted, with a wry look.

"Yet she *doesn't* know us," Mountain finally admitted. "So, it's not as if she has anything to judge by."

Sydney added, "And yet what she does know obviously has her concerned."

"The whole village is concerned too," Mountain added. "I've been there time and time again, and I don't necessarily get the cold shoulder anymore, but I really don't get a welcome either," he shared, with a shrug. "And I get it. As far as they're concerned, we're a mess out here, but, if anybody would help and tell us what they know, we would potentially get it done sooner and have much less of a mess to clean up. Instead they're all waiting for us to do it, wondering what's taking us so damn long."

"And you're still not willing to say who it is you think is behind this, are you?" Sandrine asked Mountain.

Mountain looked over at her and shook his head. "I can't yet, not in good conscience. Whoever is doing this has likely had a very long record of pulling all kinds of stunts."

"But that alone can only lead to so many options in this base," Sandrine noted, "when we're talking long term. That leaves us with Chef Elijah, possibly Joe, and then the colonel." She frowned. "And, if any of those guys are guilty, then, yeah, you better have the proof."

Teegan stared at her and didn't say anything. Then his glance went from one to the other, until Teegan shrugged. "She's not a fool."

"No, I'm not," Sandrine stated. "I do understand, but it would be nice if we could find something definitive because the atmosphere out there is ugly and getting worse by the day. And, if it is one of those three, I presume we're thinking of the Nikolai connection. Not Nikolai himself, but that this Eric guy found evidence, potentially linking someone here to Nicholai's father's murder," she suggested, with a raised eyebrow. "But, if that's the case, why would Eric do all the rest of this?"

"Therein lies the problem," Magnus pointed out. "You can have a plausible theory over one thing, but, if it doesn't relate to the other events, then it makes no sense because to think it's more than one issue is BS."

Sandrine stared at him. "Unless it's two."

He stiffened and looked at her. "Pardon?"

"A pair," she stated calmly.

Magnus frowned, but Mountain shook his head at that.

"That wouldn't make sense either."

SHE DIDN'T SAY anything, just looked back at Teegan. He was fading quickly. "And that will be enough for you," she stated, bounding to her feet. "Look at you. You're ready to collapse. Your brother can carry you back to your room, but I'm sure as hell not." Teegan glared at her, and she shook her head. "No. Enough of this he-man stuff," she said. "You have to look after yourself, or you'll end up back in that hospital bed as a patient again."

He gave her a ghost of a smile and looked over at Sydney, who was nodding vehemently.

"Sandrine's right," Sydney confirmed. "I've been watching you for the last few minutes, wondering who would carry you to your room."

Teegan stumbled to his feet and swayed. "Dammit, I figured I was doing better than that."

"You're doing how you're doing," Sandrine noted, with a gentle smile. "Even if you try to push yourself to catch up with your brother, that doesn't mean you're truly up to the task."

"I wasn't trying to catch up with him," Teegan clarified, "but, once the shooting started, I didn't want him taking a bullet. Not because of me."

Mountain said in a fury, "Don't even start talking like that. I came up here to find you, and the last thing I'll do is let a bullet take you down."

"*Great*," Teegan snapped. "So, guess what? We got a problem because I'm not about to let a bullet take you out either."

The rest of the group smiled, but Barret opened the door and suggested, "Come on. Let's get you to your room, one way or another. Mountain probably would carry you, but I know for a fact that he's pretty damn tired too, though he won't admit it."

"Of course not," Mountain snapped, as he strode out ahead of him. He looked back at his brother and asked, "You walking, or are you getting carried?"

"Walking," he declared, glaring at his brother.

And, with them heading to Teegan's room, Sandrine hopped up and followed. Teegan looked at her and asked, "Are you staying?"

"You're damn right I'm staying," she replied. "I don't like anything about your condition right now." He glared at her, and she shook her head. "No, you can put away all that macho stuff until you're a little further down the recovery line," she told him. "I wasn't expecting you to be up this long today or to put in as much hard work on your body as you've done today, much less the last few days." She took a deep breath and added, "Let's cut the crap and get you into bed."

"There are a lot better reasons to have you come spend the night. You know that, right?"

"When you feel better, we'll talk about it, but, … at the moment? Yeah, that's not happening."

And, sure enough, as they got to his room, Teegan faded even faster. He let out a strangled exclamation, as he started to fall. Luckily Mountain was right there and caught him, scooped him up, and carried him to the bed.

When Mountain looked at her with raised eyebrows, she waved him off and said, "We'll be fine." Mountain closed the door behind him on his way out. Sandrine turned and glared at Teegan. "You know you're an idiot, right?"

He gave her a ghost of a smile. "I can't be too bad though. I've still got you around."

"Ha, you wouldn't have me at all except for this posting up here," she muttered.

"Are you upset about it?" he asked, turning to face her.

"No, of course not," she murmured. "However, I would feel better if you were in better shape. You worry me."

"I'm getting better," he argued.

"No, you want to be better, but you aren't getting better, not when you keep going out on these trips."

"Maybe so, but you also know that the woman who saved my life is still out there, and I'm pretty-damn sure she needs help."

"And, if she does, how will you help her if you can't even help yourself?" Sandrine asked. "What if your brother had taken a bullet, and what if Amelia had been in that campsite, suffering in that little hidden space? You couldn't have helped either one of them, and you sure as hell couldn't have gotten yourself back safe and sound either. Think about that."

DAY 6 BEDTIME

SANDRINE KNEW SHE shouldn't have scolded Teegan, but it was damn hard not to, especially seeing him like this. By the time she got him settled into bed, he was out within seconds. She sagged onto the bed, a hand on his shoulder, as she stared down at the face that she knew so well. Yet it seemed new, unique, and different. She got up slowly and stretched, wondering if she had time to go back to her room. Was it safe or should she stay and confirm that somebody was on guard?

She didn't know how much anybody believed their assertion that the shots were trying to show them something versus taking them out, and that's what worried her. As she opened the door, she checked out into the hallway to see if anybody was there. She felt someone should stay around to keep an eye on Teegan, and, as it was, Mountain stood there on the phone.

He hung up the phone, looked at her, and asked, "What do you need?"

"To get a few things from my room for the night," she replied. "Can you keep an eye on him until I get back?" He frowned at her, and she shrugged. "I guess I'm wondering how much you really believe the shooter was showing you something versus shooting to chase you away from something."

His eyebrows shot up, and he nodded. "Good point. Go get what you need. I'll stay here."

And, with that, she headed back to her room, quickly got changed for the night and picked up a change of clothes for the morning. As she walked back down, she found Mountain on the phone again. She wasn't sure who he was talking to, but she definitely heard hard voices and tension back and forth, as information was being shared.

When he saw her, he snapped out of the call and asked, "Are you staying here for the night?"

She nodded. "I was going to, yes," she declared, a note of challenge in her voice, "unless you've got a problem with that."

He shook his head. "Nope, I sure don't. Honestly, if you weren't, I would."

She stiffened and asked, "Meaning?'

"Meaning, I don't want him alone."

"Neither do I," she agreed, as she looked in Teegan's bedroom. "He's more exhausted than I want to see."

"He's strong though," Mountain pointed out.

"He is strong, and he's very capable, and I know all that," she noted, "but he's exhausted, and I'm not sure he would wake up quickly if someone came in."

Slowly Mountain nodded. "Have you got my number?"

"I don't think so."

He gave it to her, while they were in the hallway. "If anything happens, if anything concerns you, if anything is worrisome, you contact me." And, with that, he turned and walked away.

She wasn't sure, but she felt as if it were a vote of approval in some way. Or maybe it was just because she was standing guard over his brother, so it could have been gratitude. Either way, it left a warm feeling in her heart, and, by the time she curled up in bed with Teegan, she felt a whole lot better about the whole mess.

She checked on him to ensure that he was doing okay, noting his breathing was slow and heavy. She drifted off to sleep, waking several times with a jolt, only to slide back into sleep again. Every time he was sleeping heavily beside her. Finally she drifted off to sleep. Hours later she woke, groggy, to an odd sound, thinking in the back of her mind that she heard footsteps outside in the hall.

She shifted uneasily, wondering what time it was. The footsteps weren't exactly where people would be walking past. As it was, she didn't have any reason to be alarmed, but, when they stopped outside of Teegan's room, she froze.

She picked up her phone and texted Mountain. **Is that you?**

He texted back. **What is it? What are you talking about?**

Somebody's outside our room and stopped there.

When the doorknob started to turn, she panicked, jumped to her feet, and called out, "Who's there?"

The knob froze, and the footsteps raced down the hallway.

She jerked open the door and raced down the hallway, until she heard heavy footsteps thundering behind her and then past her and beyond—Mountain now running after whoever it was too. She slowly stopped, completely out of breath, only to realize that whoever it was had somehow disappeared again.

When Mountain came back, furious, asking her what the hell happened, she was standing outside of Teegan's bedroom door. "Something woke me up, and I heard footsteps stop outside the room. When the doorknob started to turn, I called out, and they took off."

She poked her head in to confirm that Teegan was still okay, relieved to see him sleeping. The fact that he was still sleeping suddenly hit her. Something was wrong. She rushed over and checked him, but he was definitely out. Really out. She lifted his arm, dropped it, and it dropped as if a heavy weight. She turned and looked at Mountain, who was staring at her. In a harsh whisper, she said, "I think he's been drugged."

His eyebrows shot up, and he walked over and quickly checked on his brother. Then, before she had a chance to do anything, he scooped Teegan out of the bed and headed toward the medical clinic. She raced in front of them, rapping on Sydney's door when they walked past. As Sydney stumbled out of her room, still trying to keep her eyes open, she looked at Mountain carrying Teegan and then back at Sandrine.

"He's sleeping too heavily," Sandrine explained, as they all entered the clinic. Mountain placed Teegan on the nearest hospital bed. Sandrine pointed at him. "I think Teegan was drugged before he went down. We had an intruder try to come into his bedroom. I texted for help and took off after him but couldn't keep up, and he had too much of a jump on Mountain as well."

"So you didn't find him?" Magnus asked Mountain, stepping into the clinic behind them.

He shook his head. "But I have a damn good idea where he went."

"The question is, why would somebody want to come after Teegan?" Sandrine cried out.

They all shared a look, and Mountain stated, "Likely

because of whatever he found today."

"And yet you were with him," Sandrine pointed out. "Will somebody come after you?"

He gave her a ghost of a smile and nodded. "I hope so, dammit. I really hope so."

She glared at him. "That's not funny. You could be next on the list of people to go down, just like Teegan did earlier, and you won't even know when the drugs hit you."

"No, but I'll tell you one thing. It takes a hell of a lot to knock me out. And most people don't make anywhere near the right adjustments in medication doses in relation to my body weight," he shared, with a half smirk.

She stared at him intently. "So, in other words, you were probably drugged too."

He stared at her and then pivoted to look at Sydney.

She patted the second hospital bed and said, "Let's take a look. I can run some simple tests. How do you feel?"

"Mellow, tired, but it was a hard day, so that is to be expected. So, yeah, I'm tired, but I'm not stupid with it."

Magnus nodded. "To knock out Mountain would take, … Jesus, enough to knock out a horse." He grinned a bit, and then shook his head. "So, anything given to knock out Teegan here wouldn't do much to you."

"But wait," Sandrine interrupted, as she shifted to look at both brothers. "That's if the same amount was put in both foods or both drinks or whatever. What if more was put in one, and that's what Teegan got?"

Mountain frowned. "If that was so, it could kill him."

"I don't think it'll kill him," Sydney noted, a worried expression plastered on her face. "However, he's definitely out for the count, and he's staying here for the rest of the night," she declared. She looked back at the others. "How is it that somebody keeps disappearing in this base?"

"Somebody must have access to locked-off areas," Mountain suggested. "Maybe quartered off sections. I'm just starting to realize how much of this military complex is easily maneuvered around, without anybody knowing."

Magnus nodded. "It's kind of circular in construction, but hallways cross through the center," he shared. "I've got a map of it laid out, if you want to take a look."

"Oh, I definitely want to take a look," Mountain confirmed, "but I also want to make damn sure my brother's okay. And if somebody gave him a dose that was meant for me?" He shook his head. "None of us are safe anymore in this place, and I'm wondering how the hell they got us to take it."

"That's the better question," Sydney noted. "But, for now, … it would explain why Teegan's out so deeply. If anybody wanted to get something from his room or to check for something, they would want him knocked out. So, why don't you guys go figure out what it is this guy thinks he's after."

"Or if he was trying to kill Teegan," Sandrine piped up, "maybe it was too public earlier. Maybe he wanted privacy for it. Maybe he would give him another injection," she guessed. "Maybe it wasn't even related to what happened today, outside of the fact that potentially they were seen or that whoever was shooting to show them something wanted to confirm they didn't get a chance to testify."

Even as she said that, all were staring at her.

Sandrine added, "I don't know. I'm just saying options are here, and none of them are good. However, the bottom line is, you need to check your room too." She pointed at Mountain. "I don't know if they wanted you knocked out at the same time that Teegan was, but somebody came to Teegan's bedroom tonight, and they weren't expecting me to be there."

"They will know now, won't they?" Mountain stated, frowning at her.

"Yeah, they sure will," she snapped back, "and it's a damn good thing I was there."

He nodded. "I told you, if you weren't staying, I was."

"And I might have found you asleep in the hallway too," she shared. When he glared at her, she held up a hand. "Just a thought."

"Go take a look at your room and Teegan's first," Sydney stated, "and then maybe we can figure out what the hell's going on here."

At that, the men disappeared, and Sandrine sank onto a chair beside Teegan. She looked over at Sydney. "It didn't even occur to me earlier," she whispered. "He went to sleep quickly and slept soundly, but I thought he was just exhausted. When all the commotion didn't wake him up, I realized maybe it was something more and looked a little closer."

"You don't need to be blaming yourself either," Sydney said. "Once again, this is just the BS that's happening here, but it's about to come to an end."

"Why is that?"

"Because very few people have access to all the locations needed to hide in this base. That was a deliberate strategy, and now the team will take a look at what was set up, and hopefully we'll know more."

"Meaning?"

"Meaning that I believe they set up cameras, and they didn't tell anybody."

She winced. "I sure hope they aren't inside the rooms."

"No, they wouldn't be, but they are outside in the hallways, I bet," she replied cheerfully. "So, their talk about looking at things is more a case of seeing that the cameras worked."

Sandrine sighed, as she looked at Teegan. "I really want them to figure out what the hell's going on," she muttered. "This isn't exactly what I signed up for."

"Nobody did, but it doesn't matter," Sydney noted, "because hopefully it's almost over."

Nearly twenty minutes later Magnus returned, and his face was grim. Teegan was still sound asleep.

Sydney frowned at him and asked, "Anything?"

He nodded. "Yes. I won't tell you who at this point, but believe me. Things could get a little ugly right now. I want you both to stay in here and do not let Teegan out of your sight. Do you hear me?"

Both women nodded.

"Also … lock the damn door when I'm gone." He turned and left, Sydney following him, locking up behind him.

"Well, damn," Sandrine muttered. "It would be nice if he'd told us something useful."

"He's got a job to do, so he really couldn't at this point," Sydney explained. "And honestly, I'm not sure I even want to know. It'll be somebody we know, and probably somebody we weren't expecting."

DAY 7 MORNING

TEEGAN WOKE SLOWLY, his eyelids feeling as if they were made of lead, his body flushed with heat. When he finally got his eyelids to cooperate and to open wide enough to look around him, he yawned and sagged back against the bed, finding it hard to even roll over. "Man, I'm exhausted." He finally fought his eyelids and got them to stay open this time. He stared at Sandrine. "But I'm alive, and I'm okay," he replied, trying to reassure her.

She smiled and leaned over, then kissed him gently. "You are, but not necessarily the way you thought."

That didn't make any sense to him. "Sorry?"

"You were drugged last night," she said. "And, for that, I'm so sorry because I didn't recognize it right away."

He blinked at her several times. "How was I drugged?"

She gave a half smile. "That question has yet to be answered." She checked the clock. "It's six in the morning, and already chaos is happening on the base, but we're under strict orders to stay here in the medical clinic," she explained, with a cheerful smile. "So, Sydney is crashed on the bed beside you, and I'm still feeling guilty for not having figured out that you were drugged, so I've been watching over you."

He blinked several times, as he tried to process that information. "Did they find out who did it?" he asked, trying to shift upward and then groaning, as he fell back again.

"Hey, take it easy," she muttered. "It's not so much that you're injured but that it'll feel as if you are walking through molasses for a while."

He kept yawning and added, "I'm so tired."

"Yeah, that would be the drugs."

"Okay," he said, "that may very well be, but why are you under lockdown?"

"Because I guess cameras were set up that would have seen whoever I chased down the hall in the middle of the night, someone trying to get into your room," she shared.

"Whoa, whoa, whoa, whoa." He frowned at her.

"Oh, yeah, I forgot that part. Sorry." Then she launched into an explanation that had him staring at her. She shrugged. "So, you got sleep. I didn't."

"Jesus," he muttered, looking around the clinic. "No wonder you're on lockdown."

Then came a hard rap on the clinic door. Sandrine glanced over at Sydney, who was slowly waking up. She called out, "Who is it?"

"It's Mountain," came the disgruntled reply.

Sydney got up, unlocked the door, and opened it to Mountain and Magnus. As they both stepped in, Mountain walked over, took one look at his brother, and nodded with satisfaction. "Hey," he greeted him, with affection in his tone. "How're you feeling?"

"Like shit. I should feel better than this, considering I had a lot of sleep, but it doesn't feel like it was a restful sleep. Not that I haven't experienced this before."

"Drugs will do that," Mountain noted cheerfully. He looked around at the others and announced, "Okay, ... so, wait for it. ... Elijah did it."

Sandrine gasped. "What?"

Mountain nodded. "He's not telling us why and says it's not related to anything, except that he felt we needed extra rest, and we weren't getting it. I think it's a load of crock myself, but he's the one who came to your room."

"Did he say why?" Teegan asked.

"Nope, and he's not talking."

"Elijah drugged you both?" Sandrine asked. Then Sandrine nodded and answered her own question. "Of course he did. He's the only one who makes any sense."

"And yet it doesn't make any sense at all," Sydney argued, looking at them in shock. "Not to mention the fact that he's been in charge of the food this entire time. If he'd really wanted to, he could have killed all of us at any time of his choosing."

Mountain nodded slowly. "I know. So, for the moment, there's no Chef in the kitchen. Chrissy and Avalon will handle the cooking for a little bit. Nobody is saying anything, and Chef's currently in the colonel's office, where I'm guessing he'll be staying for a while."

"*Great*," Sandrine frowned. "Damn, I really like him. I didn't want him to be the bad guy."

"Of course none of us want him to be the bad guy, but it appears that he is—at least for this event." Magnus sighed. "So, the bottom line is, we still don't have all the answers, but we have some of them. Honestly, he fits and was on the list we had of suspects, and this will take us down the right pathway. Right now, I'll go grab some sleep. Breakfast will be interesting and so will lunch and dinner," he added, with a note of humor. "In the meantime, things are looking up, and we're good. So everybody can relax."

"That will make a huge difference to the atmosphere around the place," Sydney suggested. "I'm sure it will be a huge relief to everyone."

Teegan couldn't believe it. To think that Elijah was the one who had tried to get into his room and had even drugged him? It made sense in a way, because not too many people would have had access to the food, as Mountain and Teegan had arrived late for dinner, and everybody else had already eaten. It's not as if they'd served themselves. Chef had served them the food, and that's the part that really bothered Teegan.

It was way too obvious. If Chef had done it, why? And why make no attempt to hide it? Making no attempt to hide it didn't make any sense at all. Teegan shifted, realizing that he was still tired, but his mind was clearing and now raced, trying to sort it out. In a way, Elijah made a whole lot of sense.

As Teegan started to fit the pieces together, he could kind of see it. Chef was the one helping some people and dogs outside of the base. Chef was the one who often went out and sat outside or checked the generator, checked up on the guys coming and going. He had license to go into places not many people went into or had access to, and Chef was friends with Joe and had good standing with the CO as well. He could be the one behind all this.

Still disturbed by the answers, but happy to let it be the answer for now and to let go for the moment, Teegan shifted upright, looked around at Sandrine, and asked, "Breakfast?"

"I don't even know if there will be any."

Teegan laughed. "We should get there before anybody else does. There should be at least muffins."

"I'll go, and you stay here," she said. "Your mind is clearing, but you still won't be very mobile." He glared at her, and she shrugged. "Honest. I will be back soon. Sydney, are you okay here with Teegan?"

At the doc's nod, Sandrine headed to the dining room.

DAY 7 BREAKFAST

THE COFFEE WAS started, and Chrissy's shocked expression was plastered all over her face.

"I heard," Sandrine confirmed. "You need any help?"

Chrissy shook her head. "The meals for today were already set up, so I'll follow through with his plans, and we'll go from there."

"Good enough. You're not alone in here, are you?"

"No, I'm not," she said, with a casual flick of her hair. "Breakfast is due to come out in a few minutes, though I am a bit behind. Nobody cares right now anyway. I think everybody is a little too shocked to realize that Chef's under arrest."

"I don't even know if he is actually under arrest," Sandrine clarified, with a shrug. "I think we're all shocked that he had anything to do with any of this."

"And yet it's undisputed, isn't it? Whalen mentioned that Chef was caught on the video."

"I know. I heard that too," Sandrine replied, grimacing.

"Damn, what a mess," Chrissy muttered. "I'll be glad when my term here is over."

"You and the rest of us." Sandrine grabbed coffee and some muffins, then headed back.

As she walked into the clinic, Sydney left to get her breakfast. Teegan had already crashed again. Sandrine smiled and set it all down. She grabbed a muffin and sat on the other side of Teegan.

He murmured, "I'm awake." He smiled at her. "I thought I would close my eyes for a few minutes."

"That's why I went instead of you," she said.

"Anybody there?"

"Chrissy," she replied, and quickly explained the little bit she'd heard.

"Right, and that'll be the mentality from everybody right now. Not to mention a whole lot of relief that Chef didn't kill us all." Teegan nodded. "I think I'll still be feeling the effects of whatever he did to me for a while," he muttered. "Every time I try to get up, I feel as if I've got a weighted blanket on me."

She smirked. "Could be much worse. You could be six feet under. We think your dose was meant for Mountain."

He glared at her and then smiled reluctantly. "Seems we've gone through all kinds of shit already, doesn't it?"

"It sure does," she agreed, glancing at him. "As long as we're all doing okay, then it's fine."

"I think we're doing just fine," Teegan confirmed, "at least we will be, if we ever get out of here and get that chance."

"I'm hoping we will."

"Are you?" he asked suddenly. "I feel as if I'm pushing you into this."

She laughed. "I've never been one to get pushed into anything," she declared. "I always felt that we had unfinished business. as if you ducked out on me."

"I probably did. I didn't get a yes, so, in my head, you had rejected me, and I just took off," he shared.

"Yet I didn't think your marriage proposal was serious."

He smiled. "I get that. ... I definitely get it. Maybe we have a second chance coming."

"Oh, I think we do right now," she stated. "No need to wait. I feel we're here already."

"I like the sound of that," he said gently, as he looked around. "Do you think there's any chance I can go back to my room? It would be much nicer to have some private time." He waggled his eyebrows.

She snorted. "If you're talking about shenanigans in your room, I would be willing to bet that you would fall asleep before you completed anything."

He gasped at her in horror. "Don't say that. I would never live it down."

"I would never let you live it down," she vowed, with a big fat evil grin.

He rolled his eyes.

Sydney walked in just then, with a cup of coffee of her own, eyed the two of them, and nodded. "Seems you're doing better."

"Yeah," Sandrine agreed, "except Teegan says that any movement feels as if a weighted blanket were on him."

"That's the drug," the doc confirmed. "You need to sleep it off, as much as you can. You didn't ever get any quality sleep either, did you, Sandrine?"

Sandrine shook her head. "Not really. Does anyone get any sleep around this place?" she muttered.

"Those of us do, who weren't running down hallways, chasing after intruders," Sydney quipped, with a bright smile. "Go on now. The two of you, ... get lost." Sydney walked over and added, "You're free to go, but are you capable of getting up?"

He glared at the doc, hopped up, and put an arm around

Sandrine. "You grab the muffins," he murmured. "I'll need them later."

"There will be breakfast," Sandrine shared. "It'll be a little bit late this morning."

"Yeah, you mentioned that." Teegan gave her a quizzical look. "I would send you down to get more food, but I honestly think I probably need to sleep."

"I agree," she said, as she walked him slowly to his room. As they got inside, she asked him, "Are you sure you don't want to go to my room instead?"

He looked around his room and asked, "It should be okay now, right?"

"Yes, it *should* be okay," she replied. "It just feels odd."

"Your room's not that far away, if that's what you prefer."

She thought about it a moment, then shrugged. "No, this is fine. Plus, you're here already." And, with that, she helped him onto the bed. He was still in the pajamas they had gotten him into the previous night. As she sat down beside him, she handed him the muffins. "I'll go back and grab the coffee."

"If you want to go get food, I wouldn't be opposed," he said, looking hopeful.

"It might be ready. I'll go have a look." She hesitated at the doorway and looked back at him, unsure.

"I'm not going anywhere."

"I know you're not. I'm locking this. I'll be back soon."

She walked to the dining room, served up some breakfast that they could share, and with the cutlery and hot coffees on a tray, she headed back down to his room. When she called out to him, he got up and opened the door. She smiled when she saw him. "I hate to admit it, but I was a little worried you wouldn't be here."

"Oh, I get it. If the shoe were on the other foot, I would feel the same way." He curled up on the side of the bed, and the two of them slowly worked their way through breakfast. "Do you think we'll get the day off?"

"You're supposed to sleep. Doctor's orders."

"No, *you*'re supposed to sleep," he pointed out. "You're the one who stayed up all night, watching me."

"I know." She shrugged. "I am tired, and, after a big meal, I'll need to crash. Or try to at the very least."

"And that's why we're here," he said. "You need to get some rest yourself."

AND THAT'S WHAT they did. As soon as Teegan and Sandrine were done with the food, she set the tray on the floor, curled up in the bed beside him, and drifted off to sleep. He looked down at her and smiled, then wrapped his arm around her, pulled her into a spoon position, and gently fell asleep with her against him. It amazed him, as he woke the next time, how he could still feel like sleeping.

But he did, so he drifted off again, with her still sound asleep in his arms. When he woke up the third time, he felt a little more back to normal. He checked his phone and found it was almost noon. Which was damn-near amazing. He rolled over and saw her looking at him. "Hey," he said in a gentle whisper. "How are you feeling?"

"Better. How about you?"

"I'm fine," he stated, with a smile. "I was just thinking that it feels as if I'm finally getting back to normal."

"Good." She yawned. "I'm still pretty tired myself."

"Yeah, that's part and parcel of watching over someone else, isn't it?"

"I guess," she murmured, as she snuggled into the blankets. "And, if we don't have to get up, let's not."

"No, I don't think we do," he replied. "You were given the day off too."

"Uh, no, she didn't say the *day*. Sydney just said, *Go get some sleep*," Sandrine corrected.

"We don't have to tell them that we're awake, right?" Teegan teased.

She laughed at that. "I don't think that'll hold for long."

"It'll hold for a while though," he declared, as he snuggled under the covers and pulled her into his arms. "At least long enough for us to become a little more reacquainted."

As he nuzzled her neck, she laughed, looped her arms around his neck, and asked, "Just in time for you to take off again?"

"Nope, not planning on taking off again." Then he lifted his head and glared at her. "Unless … you'll reject me again."

She giggled. "Seeing how I didn't reject you then, I don't—"

"Maybe not, but it felt like it. At least that's all that settled through my drunk brain at the time," he shared, with a headshake. "Good God. The things that we do to ourselves."

"Especially when you're drunk. *So* drunk."

"Exactly." He grinned at her. "But we're smarter now."

"I don't know about that," she countered, "but definitely older. However, you were drugged this time around too." And, with peals of laughter at her own joke, she reached up and kissed him gently. He looked as if he was about to protest, when she leaned in to kiss him again. "I'm very glad you're okay," she whispered. "Whatever that last scenario was, I sure hope Chef ends up telling us what this was all about. I can't be sure because it doesn't make any sense."

"I know, but that's because nobody's had a chance to talk to him. Well, at least when they took him in, he wasn't interested in sharing."

"That was during the night though," she noted. "So who knows what's he's saying now."

Teegan nodded his agreement, saying, "True, but that's not today's issue. Today the issue is you and me."

"Oh, is that an issue now?" she asked, with interest. "And here I thought we were finally getting time for us." She was teasing him now, egging him on.

"We are together, and, no, it's not an issue. It's just time for us to be alone." He leaned over and gave her a big, loud, smacking kiss.

Chuckling, she wrapped her arms around him and pulled him down on top of her. "Surely you can do better than that."

"*Ha*. What if my brain's still rattled, and I can't do very well at all?"

"In that case, I'll just have to tease you about it unmercifully later."

In mock outrage, he leaned back, then looked at her and chuckled. "No, that won't be necessary." And, when he lowered his head the next time, he delivered a kiss that curled her toes.

DAY 7 NOON

SANDRINE SIGHED HAPPILY in Teegan's arms, as he deepened the kiss again and again, until she was gasping for more. When he finally lifted his head, she muttered, "I forgot how good that was with you."

"I aim to please," he said, as he nuzzled her cheek, then down to her ear and along the side of her throat.

"Sometimes, there's making love, and sometimes there's having sex," she whispered in between her moans and her giggles. "Both are good, depending on the circumstance, but some of it's definitely better."

He nodded. "Making love is with somebody you care about," he admitted. "And that's always been my preference."

"Yeah, you and me both," she agreed, as she tapped him on the nose. "But I do want to remind you that we might end up losing our privacy at any moment."

"Oh, I see." He chuckled. "I get it now. You're in a rush and want me to believe it has everything to do with a time frame."

She rolled her eyes. "There *could* be a time frame issue." She took a deep breath and then drew closer to him. "I would hate to be interrupted now."

He nodded. "I hear you there, and unfortunately, being in the position we currently find ourselves, ... well, ...

something like that could happen."

"It absolutely could," she agreed, with a broad smile, as she nudged him gently with her hips. He bent his head and this time kissed her with enough power to leave her quaking in the bed, her heart slamming against her chest. "Jesus, when you go from zero to sixty, you really mean it, don't you?"

"Absolutely," he said, with a knowing smile, as he kissed her deeply again and again, until she was quivering.

Careful of his still-healing wounds, he shifted slowly, until he was atop her. She opened her thighs wide to welcome him, but instead he slowly worked his way down her body, leaving her crying out. Realizing the noise she was making, he rose up, kissed her, and then placed her own hand against her own mouth, so that she wouldn't cry out as he returned to exploring her body.

By the time he finally rose to give her another tongue-lashing, deep-throated kiss, she was more than ready, her thighs wrapped tightly around his hips. As he settled himself at the heart of her, with one push he was seated deep within. He waited, his forehead against hers, gentle kisses on her lips and tongue, as she shivered in his arms. "Are you okay?" he whispered.

She nodded and wrapped her arms tighter around his neck. "I am absolutely perfect."

And, with that, he started to move.

When she came apart in his arms soon afterward, the surge had happened so fast and with such force that she could hardly do anything, as he rode her through it, until he reached his own climax. Gasping in his arms, she didn't even know what to say.

He whispered to her, "Jesus, I can't believe I'd forgotten."

She nodded. "I'm not sure that even back then it was ever this good."

"That's what I was wondering myself," he murmured. "It seems so damn special right now."

"Aside from the fact that you almost didn't survive, and we're in a place where so many people haven't," she murmured, "anything wonderful like this right now is damn special. Plus to have found you again after all this time and to know that you still cared?" She shook her head. "That's a miracle."

With a smile on his lips, he rolled over, curled her up close against him, and whispered, "Sometimes some things are meant to be. This time it absolutely is." He kissed her again. "Now one more little nap, and then we'll have to rejoin the real world."

"A nap it is." Sandrine yawned, then, curling up in his arms, they both fell asleep.

EPILOGUE

P UZZLED, MOUNTAIN STARED at Chef Elijah. "None of us can figure out why. Why would you do such a thing?" he asked the big, likable man.

Chef shrugged, didn't say anything, and crossed his arms over his chest. He remained silent.

"See? It doesn't make sense. There's no motive. There's absolutely nothing. I don't have a clue why you would even try to knock out Teegan."

"Not saying nothing," Elijah replied through gritted teeth.

Then the door opened, and the colonel stepped in. Mountain stood and tilted his head. "Sir."

"Did you get any answers from him?"

"No, not yet," he replied in frustration.

The CO looked over at Elijah, disappointment evident in his expression. "I don't know what the hell you've been playing at or how long you've been at it," he muttered, "but you've sure as hell disappointed a lot of people."

Elijah closed his eyes and didn't say anything. Mountain watched the two of them, sensing a way-bigger betrayal happening here, as Chef and the CO had been friends for a very long time.

"I'm sorry, sir. He doesn't want to talk, and I've been at it for a couple hours now," Mountain confirmed, as he stretched his large frame.

"Oh, I can talk to him," the colonel declared. "Might be the best thing for both of us. We go way back."

"Not alone, sir," Mountain noted, a warning in his tone.

The CO nodded. "No, of course not." He glared at Elijah. "A damn nuisance this is," he muttered. "And here I was looking forward to my breakfast."

"We can't let him back into the kitchen, not after …"

The colonel shot a hard look at their beloved and trusted chef and then left the room.

Mountain shook his head at Chef. "I don't know what the hell's going on here," he admitted in a low voice, "but I don't believe it for one second."

"Mountain!" The shout came from the other side of the door. As he stepped out to the hallway, leaving a guard on Elijah, Magnus raced toward him. "What's up?" Mountain asked, with a fierce gaze.

"You've got a visitor," he said, "and unfortunately she's hurt."

His eyebrows shot up. "She? Who is it?"

"It's Amelia," Magnus confirmed, as excitement filled his voice—panic too. "She got here on her own, but she's hurt, and she's hurt bad. I've got her in with Sydney, but you need to come—now."

This concludes Book 7 of Shadow Recon: Teegan.
Read about Mountain: Shadow Recon, Book 8

Shadow Recon: Mountain (Book #8)

Deep in the permafrost of the Arctic, a joint task force, comprised of over one dozen countries, comes together to level up their winter skills. A mix of personalities, nationalities, and egos bring out the best—and the worst—as these globally elite men and women work and play together. They rub elbows with hardy locals and a group of scientists gathered close by …

One fatality is almost expected with this training. A second is tough but not a surprise. However, when a third goes missing? It's hard to not be suspicious. When the missing man is connected to one of the elite Maverick team members and is a special friend of Lieutenant Commander Mason Callister? All hell breaks loose …

Mountain hit the Arctic, knowing full well they would have to drag his dead body back out of the tundra before he ever quit on his little brother, Teegan. Theirs hadn't been the easiest of upbringings, but, when times had been tough, there'd always been the two of them.

Yet the series of events so far has gone from mysterious to downright deadly, and just what is the elusive Dr. Amelia's part in all this anyway? Like a ghost, she slips in and around everyone. What is her problem with the base, and, more important, what is her end game?

Dr. Amelia Morrison had seen too much in her life to trust anything she can't fathom with her own eyes. So, what she sees here makes no sense. Something is rotten at the Arctic international military training camp. She needs to stay close, but, deep inside, she just wants to run for cover. But this mountain of a man keeps her coming back, and his younger brother she manages to keep alive. However, saving a man out in these harsh elements is a completely different story than saving him from his fellow man.

Together, Mountain and Amelia need to solve this nightmare, before no one else is left alive …

Find Book 8 here!
To find out more visit Dale Mayer's website.
https://geni.us/DMSSRMountain

Author's Note

Thank you for reading Teegan: Shadow Recon, Book 7! If you enjoyed the book, please take a moment and leave a short review.

Dear reader,

I love to hear from readers, and you can contact me at my website: www.dalemayer.com or at my Facebook author page. To be informed of new releases and special offers, sign up for my newsletter or follow me on BookBub. And if you are interested in joining Dale Mayer's Reader Group, here is the Facebook sign up page.
http://geni.us/DaleMayerFBGroup

Cheers,
Dale Mayer

About the Author

Dale Mayer is a *USA Today* best-selling author, best known for her SEALs military romances, her Psychic Visions series, and her Lovely Lethal Garden cozy series. Her contemporary romances are raw and full of passion and emotion (Broken But … Mending, Hathaway House series). Her thrillers will keep you guessing (Kate Morgan, By Death series), and her romantic comedies will keep you giggling (*It's a Dog's Life*, a stand-alone novella; and the Broken Protocols series, starring Charming Marvin, the cat).

Dale honors the stories that come to her—and some of them are crazy, break all the rules and cross multiple genres!

To go with her fiction, she also writes nonfiction in many different fields, with books available on résumé writing, companion gardening, and the US mortgage system. All her books are available in print and ebook format.

Connect with Dale Mayer Online

Dale's Website – www.dalemayer.com
Twitter – @DaleMayer
Facebook Page – geni.us/DaleMayerFBFanPage
Facebook Group – geni.us/DaleMayerFBGroup
BookBub – geni.us/DaleMayerBookbub
Instagram – geni.us/DaleMayerInstagram
Goodreads – geni.us/DaleMayerGoodreads
Newsletter – geni.us/DaleNews